Mercy in a Red Cloak

D0746117

By Carrie Fancett Pagels

Hearts Overcoming Press

Carrie Fancett Pagels

Mercy in a Red Cloak

Dedication

This story is dedicated to Dr. Phil Porter, Director of Mackinac State Historic Parks, for his tireless work in bringing the Straits of Mackinac to "life" for visitors.

Acknowledgements

I always want to give thanks to God for making this story possible, and all of my books which He has graciously given me. Much appreciation to my son, Clark J. Pagels, for his patience and persistence helping me and encouraging me as I've worked on this story.

I'm grateful to my longtime critique partner, the incredible author Kathleen L. Maher, for her assistance. Thank you to Anne Payne, a real "trooper", who served as a Beta reader for this story in its original version. Thank you also to my wonderful current Beta readers for the substantially revised version, Andrea Stephens especially for your eye for detail and Joy Ellis for your encouragement. You all bless me with your help!

I've been blessed by the Mackinac State Historic Parks staff and volunteers who have answered my many questions over the years when I've visited.

My Pagels' Pals members, a group of about ninety readers who support my writing ministry, have given me support and prayers and so much more over the years, and I am truly grateful.

Author's Notes

Having grown up in Michigan's Eastern Upper Peninsula, and having visited Fort Michilimackinac many times, I was familiar with the story of Pontiac's Rebellion. Fast forward many decades to when I began the Colonial Quills blog and I began thinking again about this uprising. Honestly, I'd not realized that it was a concerted attack across a large area of many frontier forts. I'd mostly considered it a local or regional attack on Michigan forts. Fort Detroit was attacked first, at the beginning of May, and then Fort Michilimackinac was attacked in early June.

An author often asks "What if?" questions. While working on a novel, now published as *Saving the Marquise's Granddaughter*, I created the character Shadrach Clark. Shad has subsequently appeared in my novella, "Shenandoah Hearts", in *The Backcountry Brides Collection*, too. I have an unpublished novel, also, in which he played an important part, but *Mercy in a Red Cloak* was written all for Shad. I'd asked myself, 'What if my hero was one of the people who tried to warn the commanders at both Michigan forts?' So, this story was born from that question.

I also wondered what kind of romantic interest would be "right" for Shad. I'd married him off to a beautiful Chippewa woman when he was young, but this wife later dies. I wanted a new romantic interest who would also reach that spiritual part of him that had been squelched. In researching my own genealogy, I'd discovered a Methodist church deacon who lived in the wilds of North Carolina near the time frame of this book. I've always been interested in "Circuit Riders" or clergymen who traveled up and down the Great Wagon Road to bring the Gospel. So, in wondering what kind of woman might possibly be a match for a widowed frontier scout, I created Mercy, the daughter of a circuit rider pastor.

Scouts suffered very difficult lives. I researched through many books on colonial era scouts and also delved through stories in the Rare Books Library at the University of Virginia, to get a sense of Shad's character. I also read numerous books about colonial era scouts, in particular Simon Kenton. My bookshelves have also been crammed with purchases from the Mackinac State Historic Parks, recounting life during the time frame of this novella.

This story was originally begun almost a decade ago. Since that time, I have published many stories set in the area of the Straits of Mackinac and Mackinac Island. One of my characters, Maude Welling, from Maggie Award winning *My Heart Belongs on Mackinac Island*, has a grandmother named Jacqueline. You'll find Jacqueline's own grandmother, albeit a little girl, in this story! I hope those of you who enjoyed Maude's story, and who "met" Jacqueline more fully in "The Sugarplum Ladies" in *The Victorian Christmas Brides Collection*, will enjoy learning a little more about their fictional "family history".

This story is fictional. Although I have some real-life characters mentioned, I've added fictional elements. The real-life Jean-Baptiste Cadotte and his wife were highly influential leaders in both Sault Sainte Marie and in the Straits of Mackinac and they did provide protection to some of the English. British officer John Jamet suffered significant burns in the Sault Sainte Marie fort fire and later returned to Fort Michilimackinac and was present during the attack. Cadotte's Native American wife was reportedly related to Madjeckewiss who was one of the leaders of the attack on Fort Michilimackinac. The Michilimackinac fort commander, Captain George Etheridge, was by all historical accounts too proud or ignorant to listen to warnings from others that his men were at risk. The children of French soldiers at Fort Michilimackinac before the French-Indian war show in the records of infants baptized at the fort. That notation in the registry of one such baptism of an officer's child got me thinking about what if – what if that baby was kidnapped? Fictional Jacqueline was born of that question. So, the real-life family of Commander Beaujeu de Villemonde never experienced the tragedy that I inflicted upon them (to my knowledge.)

There's so much wonderful history in the Straits of Mackinac. I encourage you to visit the book stores at the Mackinac State Historic Parks on Mackinac Island and in Mackinaw City for a large selection of nonfiction books and also the Island Bookstore for fiction and nonfiction set in the area. Also, the libraries on Mackinac Island and in Mackinaw City have wonderful reference materials.

Prologue
Outside Germantown, PA—June 1753

Mercy Clarke fingered the broach at her neckline, a token of Amos's promise as he hopped into his parent's buggy, then drove off without looking back. Would Amos wear a beard this time next year as was the Amish custom—and could she abandon her own faith so they might marry? Mercy pulled her fraying brown wool cloak tighter around her neck, her knuckles brushing the pin, its bar pricking her fingers.

She cried out and released her hold, a streak of blood crossing her fingertips.

Nearby, in the barn, her father curried his horse. She couldn't break Father's heart. As a Methodist pastor, a circuit-rider whose reputation was growing, she'd played with fire by encouraging Amos' affections.

Father's cautionary words, spoken earlier in the day echoed in her mind. "He's in his *rumspringa*, Mercy—remember well."

She shivered, trying to shake off the sensation of an oncoming storm. Perhaps it was the attacks on other settlements that put her on edge. She'd never had to flee to a fort for protection—not yet.

Cool twilight air urged her toward the cozy interior of the stone house, but she resisted, instead seating herself on the stoop. She waited for her father, who'd disappeared inside the barn.

Crickets called to one another as the breeze rustled the new leaves on the trees. Hoofbeats announced a visitor diverting from the road onto their property. A young man, with hair as golden as Amos's, yanked his mount to a halt. He leapt from the horse and tied its leads to their hitching post. Mercy's heart kicked up a notch. Dressed in buckskins, reddish-gold whiskers dotted the lower half of the stranger's handsome face.

Mercy rose, alarm rising as the man strode toward her. She moved onto the grass and peered toward the barn door where her father moved to grab his rifle. Father may be a preacher, but one would have to be daft to ignore the dangers on the frontier.

"Is this the Clark home?" the stranger called out. He moved within a stone's throw away.

Mercy searched the young man's lean face for recognition but couldn't place him. "Yes."

He moved closer. "Rachel Clarke?" His blue-green gaze darted from her hair, to her eyes, nose, and mouth and then up and down her. She flushed with embarrassment.

Rachel was indeed her given name, although she went by Mercy. She dipped her chin.

His Adam's apple bobbed "Reverend Jon Clarke's daughter?"

She rubbed her arms beneath the wool cape. "Yes."

"You've finally come from London?" He stared at her, his mouth slightly agape.

"We did." A year earlier, when her mother had died.

A huge grin split the man's face and tears glistened in his eyes—lighting his strong features. "I can't believe it, after all these years."

Mercy frowned. The family's move had been an impulsive one, and a decision that had brought much peril.

The man took two steps closer. "Thank God it's true. Rachel—don't you know me?"

No, she didn't—would have remembered such a striking man.

"It's me Shadrach—your brother!"

She had no brother.

He drew closer and brushed the hair back from her brow, sending warmth through her. He frowned and abruptly stepped away from her, his eyes full of despair.

Trembling, Mercy wrapped her arms around her middle as Father stepped out, his rifle at the ready.

"I have no son." The man of middling years narrowed his gaze at Shad and kept his gun trained on him.

Shad raised his hands.

Crushing affirmation in his chest verified Shad's mistake. "I...I am Shadrach Clark, here to see if it was true that my sister and father—"

"I'm Reverend Jonathan Clarke—we spell Clark with an 'e' at the end—and this is my daughter Rachel Mercy—most folks around here call her Mercy. And I have no son—only the one child."

"I'm sorry." Shad stared down at his moccasins, dirty from the days of walking before he'd obtained a mount. "My father is Reverend John Clark—no 'e' at the end, and plain John not Jonathan."

The pretty girl, whom he'd prayed could be his younger sibling, squeezed his hand.

"Your sister is Rachel, also? And your father clergy?"

He met her soft gaze. "Yes."

The preacher rocked on his heels and lowered his gun. "I am sometimes called Jon, as an abbreviation for my given name. I can see where the mistake could be made."

Common enough names, John and Rachel Clark, but when the trusted scout Kennett told him of the preacher and his daughter and described them, Shad made haste to return from his militia mission in the Shenandoah Valley. Hope had fueled his journey, though doubt had dogged every mile. But he'd so wanted to believe he'd finally found them.

"My mother's name is Anne." Saying the name made her seem more real—not a distant memory of a beautiful woman crying at the port in London as she waved goodbye.

"Julia was my wife's name. And I'm sorry for this confusion." The clergyman's brows knit together in concern.

Shad inhaled the deep scent of fresh-tilled Pennsylvania soil. "Six years ago, my father and mother sent me ahead of them to the colonies…"

Six long years. The recollection of their parting at the London wharf, Rachel clinging to his mother's hand, knifed his heart in recollection. "I set off with my aunt and uncle—also a preacher, and I was to await my parents and sister's arrival."

The young woman flinched when he ran a thumb over the smooth flesh atop it.. The young woman's eyes widened, and he released her hand.

This Rachel, named *Mercy* rather, possessed an angel's face awash with sadness. Her eyes reflected a knowing grief. "So long ago—yet your parents never arrived?"

He cringed. "Seems a lifetime ago."

He'd been twelve. Before the horror of his uncle's and cousin's deaths aboard ship. Before his aunt's horrible new husband hauled them off to the Shenandoah Valley. Before they'd been attacked by a rogue tribe. And before he'd been rescued and brought to Michilimackinac to live among the Chippewa. Where he'd return to again, the scout who was a failure when it came to tracking his own kin.

"Mercy girl, put the kettle on the fire and let's offer tea to our guest."

"I don't wish to trouble you."

"No trouble at all. Is it Mercy?"

Shad had scouted this Pennsylvania village before, a growing community of mainly Palatinaters and Amish folk. Not many English like these two. Their sturdy home sat at the edge of the community, which circled a central area where farmer's met for market each week. The close proximity of mainly farms also served to provide protection in the case of Indian attack.

Mercy smiled shyly up at Shad. "We're happy to have company, even if by mistake."

Reverend Clarke cocked his head. "I don't believe in mistakes. God always brings good out of difficult situations, to those who love Him."

How could a God who loved him have taken his family from Shad? Little Fawn and her people would be his family now. But he'd not share his views with this preacher.

"Father, we're not at one of your stump meetings."

Stump meetings? "You're a circuit rider, sir?"

The man beamed broadly. "I am."

"And your daughter accompanies you?" Shad couldn't imagine such a thing but the words had slipped from his lips.

"On occasion, but mostly she remains here to look after our home. Such a good girl she is."

The young woman was no girl. Worry tugged at her brows but she said nothing.

Shad swallowed hard. He passed this way regularly, at least twice a year. This may not be his sister, but she bore looking after.

Much later, after a hearty meal of stewed pork, biscuits, and peach compote, all of Shad's fears had been confirmed. Reverend Clarke, whose good sense may have left him after his wife's death, allowed his daughter to live alone while he traveled. Although they had many good neighbors, there was no other family. With her sweetness and beauty, hopefully some frontiersman would take her as wife and protect her. Something in her eyes hinted that she had a beau. Still. . .

He'd ask his friend Colonel Christy and his son William to check in on them from time to time. And Shad would make sure he did, too. Then in a year or two, when Mercy was settled in with a husband, that would be her spouse's duty. That husband would be a lucky man. Did Little Fawn think the same of Shad – that she was lucky? What did he, as a scout, have to offer?

Chapter 1

Nine Years Later, Autumn, 1762

The frontier Pennsylvania village had grown much in the years that Shad had traversed the area. One thing had not wavered – his friendship with Mercy and her father. The Clarkes had become almost like family to him, definitely the closest of trusted companions. This year, since his wife's death, he'd returned four times. Something inside him drew him back to the cottage at the edge of the settlement. Was it the preacher's words, so much like his father's or was it the man's daughter? When Little Fawn had died, his first thought had been to flee to where the Clarkes would offer him solace. And they hadn't disappointed him that summer – sheltering him in a cocoon of kindness and sympathy. And since that time, a different kind of hope had grown in his heart, one he wasn't sure Mercy returned.

"Ho the house!" he called out as he approached.

The tawny homespun curtains at the windows parted, and Reverend Clarke peered out.

The door flew open and Mercy stood framed there, her face welcoming him back. When her father joined her, a pang of regret settled in Shad's chest. Mercy took care of her father. Who would do so if she returned Shad's feelings? If she came with him? And where would they go?

"Welcome, friend!" Reverend Clarke linked his arm through Mercy's and drew her forward into the yard. "Let me help you with your horse."

As he customarily did, the pastor embraced him and clapped his back before leading Shad's mount away.

Mercy stood in the yard, hands clasped at her waist. He longed to hold her in his arms and tell her what a good

14

woman she was. Time for that later.

As he took two steps closer to her, Mercy's cheeks bloomed a deep pink. Her behavior toward him had altered since his wife's death. Did she look at him as he now did her, with something more than friendship blossoming? Something more than the sisterly affection she'd professed?

"Shad, we're so glad you've come again. And so soon after the last visit." If possible, her blush deepened.

Unlike with his Native Chippewa wife, Mercy would not likely announce that she had chosen him as husband. And his skills with courting were weak to nil. "I'm mighty glad to be here, Mercy. And I've brought you and your father some gifts." He always did.

"You're so good to us, Shad." She smiled. Why hadn't he noticed how beautiful she was when she smiled? Perhaps because it was safe to admit the thought now.

He swallowed hard. He'd led a hard life and likely would continue to do so. Why did he think it would be right to even consider asking this dear friend of his to consider him as something more?

Later that night, over a savory dinner of venison, root vegetables and cornbread, Shad caught Mercy's furtive glances. When her father retired to bed, they sat in the parlor, a lamp casting a golden glow over the rag rug on the wood floor.

"My father is venturing out further on his missions than I'm comfortable with, Shad." Her eyes pleaded with him to help.

"Aye, and I heard you tell him of your concerns." Shad brushed a lock of hair back from his forehead.

"And he ignored my fears."

As he always had.

If Mercy knew of a fraction of the dangers that Shad

faced in his scouting, she'd be horrified. No, his plan, his thoughts that she might be able to live in his world were only dreams. But being with her, he had no doubt that he loved her. And he loved her too much to bring her North, to his home. Could he give up his life as a scout? And what if she did not return his feelings?

There was a way to find out.

April, 1763

Where is Father? Holding back the tawny homespun curtains, Mercy peered out the mullioned lead-glass window at the road. Her father had traveled down the Great Wagon road two months earlier, to a stump meeting further into the Shenandoah Valley. Why did she think by standing here that she could summon him back? The treaty with the French to end the war, signed in February, had allowed their friend Colonel Lee Christy to send several of his scouts to search out Mercy's father. Even Christy's son, William, a close friend of Shad's. But they'd not sent word.

A wagon rolled up the road, a blond-haired man driving. Amos Scholtus, now one of the Amish deacons, and the father of seven little sons, directed the horses near the barn and pulled to a stop. He was still her best friend's brother, and he'd been stopping to help her with the more physical tasks—toil she'd been unable to accomplish without Father at home. Amos glanced toward the window and waved to her. Then he turned away. Mercy watched as his broad shoulders heaved as he tossed hay bales down from his buggy. Although Amos had been faithful in helping her, it was unlikely that his wife would allow him to continue much longer. Not that his wife was supposed to know about Mercy and Amos's courting days—but she did. Everyone seemed to know about the preacher's daughter who'd almost joined the Amish.

Her courtship with Amos had been decidedly different from the friendship over the past ten years that had grown between her and Shad Clark. Several times each year the famous scout made a trek through Pennsylvania, always stopping at their home. Shad had married a native woman during that time. Then, this past year with his wife having died, things had changed.

Mercy sighed then turned to the pot of beans and ham cooking over coals in the hearth. Worry bubbled right along with her meal. No word from Shad as to his arrival at the fort at Michilimackinac and Father still missing. She gritted her teeth. With what coin she had, she'd need to make plans to leave soon before winter set in. Had she misunderstood the promise in Shad's kiss and in his words? His unexpected visit had taken her off-guard. As had his many questions about what she wanted to do with her life. She wanted a husband, children, and a home—but she'd not confessed all that to him.

Amos didn't bother to come up to the house before he left. Just as well. He left her alone. Alone with no husband or father. Alone with no children of her own. But when she dreamt of children now, they all looked like a certain golden-haired scout. A little blond girl sometimes skipped through her daydreams. She wiped away a tear and set about her tasks.

After Mercy accomplished her daily chores and hung her washtub up on the house's exterior wall. The sun set behind the vast tree line.

From the south, dust flew up on the road. In the distance, two bedraggled men rode in on dun-colored horses. Their faces loosely covered with thin cloth, suggested they'd ridden a far distance. Or were they trying to conceal their identities?

The horses whinnied and stomped as they approached. Fear crept up Mercy's arms like spiders from a woodpile, as she headed inside and reached for the gun by the door. A woman at the edge of town, by herself—what was she thinking? Should have stayed in town with her friend, Lena, and her family. Right near Amos and his growing brood. Right where she could fully sense what an old maid she'd become as she quilted with Lena and her large family. Although the riders appeared familiar, she was unsure so Mercy closed the door and grabbed the plank that served to bar the door.

As she was about to set the wooden board down hard into the metal braces to latch the door, one of the men called out, "Ho, the house! It's Christy and son, Miss Clarke!"

Mercy exhaled a slow breath and released it, lowering the plank and setting it back against the wall, then opened the door fully. These two men were Shad's closest companions and frequent visitors to their home. She'd told them on their last visit, a month earlier, about her father's disappearance.

"We have new mounts but it's still us!" William's shy smile and Colonel Christy's cockeyed grin brought tears to her eyes. She ran to the men and threw her arms around the silver-haired officer's neck, inhaling his bayberry scent. Christy held himself straight and did not return her impulsive gesture. She pulled back and crossed her arms, tears trickling down her cheeks.

"Do you have word of Father?" Pray God such good news was the reason for their arrival.

When the Christy men exchanged glances, she

swallowed. *Not good news.*

Brushing dirt from his buckskins, William strode toward her. "Nothing, Mercy—can't find him anywhere between here and Charlottesville."

"What about Shad?" She raised her clasped hands to her mouth.

The scout stopped. "I'd hoped you had word."

She lowered her hands. "Not since last month."

William shook his head. "So, Father's most valuable scout, Shadrach Clark, is yet unaccounted for."

The senior Christy joined them. "Shad vanished after reporting to Fort Detroit about a month ago. He failed to make contact with the Michilimackinac post."

"That is about the same time Father was supposed to return." Were the two events connected?

"I know Shad has stopped here regularly—pretty much every autumn and sometimes in spring."

"And more", she wanted to say, but bit her tongue.

William's rosy cheeks attested to the cool evening air setting in. "Did he say anything to you about his plans now that the war has ended?"

Mercy's mouth opened but she couldn't tell them what she *inferred* Shad to say—that he wished for her to start a new life with him. They'd talked so much and he'd asked so many questions. Yet he'd never come out and asked her the particular question lingering between them.

Shad was upset, of course, because Little Fawn had died, but he'd said he'd made peace with his loss and was ready to move on again with his life. Implying, she thought, with her.

"Mind if I get some fresh water from the well, Mercy?" William's dark eyes, the ones her friend in Virginia, Sarah Rousch, so admired, met hers only briefly before he strode to the table.

Sarah and William had now been married over seven years and produced three sturdy boys during the time when all Mercy had accomplished was to care for her father.

William retrieved a pitcher. He grinned. "It's the one Shad and I traded for two summers ago!"

"Indeed, it is." She returned his smile, remembering how proud Shadrach had been to offer the sturdy vessel to her father and her as a gift of friendship—a reminder that he considered them dearest companions, almost like family.

William slapped a hand against the side of the vessel. "Those French voyageurs at Michilimackinac had no idea who we were—two scouts for their enemy."

She frowned. Shad lived amongst the Chippewa people of the north. Even during the war with the French, he'd not been harmed, though he'd secretly scouted for the English. 'Twas a miracle. His parents had named him rightly – like Shadrach who with Meshach and Abednego came through the fire.

"Good thing they mistook you both for Frenchmen." Colonel Christy ran long fingers along the back of a rush-seated chair. Mercy had repaired that very chair with Shad's help the previous year.

"I'm not sure they cared about anything other than trading their furs, though." William smiled wryly.

"Sit down—you must be hungry." Beans, ham, cornbread and cheese were all she had at hand, and she gathered them up from the cupboard nearby and transferred them to the table.

"Sir, might you and William stay?" She eyed Father's open bedroom door. "'Twould be good to have company." Men's company—two people she knew could protect her if need be.

Her friend Lena had passed along rumors that there was unrest among the Indians at the border of Pennsylvania.

The older man bent to rub his booted leg. She'd polish and buff his boots for him later—knew how he loved to keep them spotless.

"Take off your boots, Colonel Christy, and relax. Do you need help?"

First one fine ebony and contrasting brown leather boot clomped to the floor, then the other.

Mercy laughed. "If only your dogs were here—you'd feel right at home, wouldn't you?"

His rich laugh joined hers. "I would. I miss my rascals—though not their baying. But Rosa has them with her."

Rosa, his gypsy woman. Mercy's cheeks heated and she turned to retrieve two plates from the rack over the dry sink and some utensils. It wasn't her concern what the colonel's relationship with Rosa was. Some said he still had a legal wife.

Lee Christy dragged his seat closer to the table. "Mercy, what have you heard from Shad?"

Heat flowed up from her chest to join the twin torches in her cheeks. "About a month ago he visited."

Shad had kissed her for the very first time and in that kiss, she'd sensed an unasked question. But he'd not written her since. *What a silly fool I was, thinking that he wanted more than friendship—marriage even.*

Embarrassment kept her back turned from the colonel as she gathered up utensils and cloths. Did he know that Shad had avoided her since then?

"We've no report from Shad after he arrived at Fort Detroit last month." The bite in his voice could have cut through the salted and smoked ham on the counter.

And she'd had no word of Father. If her father didn't

return, she'd have to assume him to be dead.

"He normally would send me a note from the fort when he passed through. But not this time." Moisture filmed her eyes as she plucked the creamware plates and brought them to the table.

"Why mightn't he send you word?"

Was it because he wished to hide from her? Did Shad regret their moment of intimacy in the barn before he left? She squared her shoulders and brought the dinnerware to the table. "I don't know. I was hoping you'd heard something."

Lines formed on Colonel Christy's smooth forehead. Although his hair was silver, she knew he was much younger than he appeared, despite now being a grandfather many times over. An aristocrat, with a grand home in Philadelphia, he nonetheless acted much like the other rugged frontiersmen who passed through. His son, who stood to inherit his father's fortune, likewise often arrived in buckskins and had not a haughty attitude in his body.

William pushed through the door with his shoulder and then closed it with a kick. His father cleared his throat. After setting the water jug atop the table, the dark-eyed man returned to the door and lowered the latch.

"I'll curry the horses *after* we quench our thirst, Father." Brushing back his black queue, William winked at her. "And after we eat. I'm starving."

"You might wish to put this up." Colonel Christy lifted her small pouch from the table and held it out to Mercy.

"Thank you." She turned and laid it atop the mantel. That slight bag held the parishioners' contributions to her home—which were rapidly dwindling. With only the root vegetables from her garden and what she'd put up for winter she couldn't survive alone without additional funds.

She had no one to turn to. But what could she do?

She set the table and soon they were settled for their meager meal.

"We're going to have to go north and find Shad." Colonel Christy began ladling the beans and meat onto his and William's plates, then hesitated, looking to Mercy for affirmation.

She nodded as his cheeks reddened. The colonel had already become too accustomed to his backwoods ways when away from military life. What was he like at home in Philadelphia with his fine manor, porcelain, and silver and his many servants to wait upon him and William? Embarrassment heated her own face. Beans and pork. But 'twas all she had to offer.

"Far north." William's black eyes met his father's silver gaze. "Straits of Mackinac."

Mercy pushed the crock of butter and the cornbread toward the men and then settled her skirts around her on the bench at the end of the square table.

"Why now?"

The colonel's lips drew in tight. "Trouble brewing—the natives aren't happy with how the fort commander is treating them. They miss the French—and their gifts."

William snorted. "And they're treated disrespectfully."

As he lifted his fork to his mouth, Mercy cleared her throat. "I'll say a brief prayer."

The young man shoved the roast ham in his mouth.

Mercy laughed, bowed her head and closed her eyes. "Lord, bless this humble meal and bring safety to us and to my father...and Shad. In Jesus's name, amen." Her throat clogged with swallowed tears.

"Amen," the Christy men echoed. Then both dug into their food.

Mercy took a small bite and swallowed. "By the looks of both you and your horses, you seem to have ridden hard to get here."

"The matter is urgent. We must find Shad." Colonel Christy's gray eyes appeared almost colorless in the candlelight.

William spoke around a mouthful, "We're worried about him. And the coming trouble."

She glanced toward the mantel where a decade of Shad's gifts and trinkets brought color, and to the hook upon which her old red cloak from him hung. Father couldn't convince her to cut it into rags. 'Twas too precious to her— Shad's first gift to her after he'd returned the following year after he'd first met them.

"What kind of trouble do you mean?"

Father and son exchanged glances. "We need our best scout. And I need to share information with the commanders at both forts."

Shad had spoken of how the forts, now taken over by the English, could benefit from women like her with good skills at stitching and quilting. 'Twould be a way she could support herself if her father didn't return.

"Can I come with you? Shad asked me to come to the fort." 'Twasn't exactly the truth, but she wasn't going to confide in them that he had all but offered her marriage at their last visit. And he had previously asked what she thought of coming to nearby Fort Michilimackinac—that the English soldiers would benefit from a preacher if her father felt so led to make the move. Which he hadn't.

Colonel Christy's eyebrows arched high.

His son's grin turned cocky. "Perhaps Shad thought he could find you a husband at one of the forts."

So, Shad hadn't told them of any plans for him and her.

Mercy's pewter utensil clattered to her plate, spattering her meal across her bodice. Only several years her junior, William, too, considered her in desperate need of a husband.

The colonel wiped at his mouth. "William, your words are insufferably rude—apologize at once." The young man's eyes bore into his father's, but softened as he turned to face Mercy. She stopped dabbing at her face with the cloth.

William sighed. "I'm sorry, Miss Clarke, but Shad has always said you were too pretty to be . . ." Halting, William's cheekbones began to appear rosy in the bright beeswax candlelight.

His father chuckled. "Indeed, my son is correct. Shad has opined you to be too lovely to be unmarried so long and said repeatedly that had you been brought near any of the officers you'd be married off before a fortnight passed."

Shad had never said as much to her. So, he didn't wish to marry her—only to introduce her to someone who would. Why had he kissed her then? Two tiny tears insistently pushed out from her eyes. Twin sentinels of more to come.

"It's a hard trip, make no mistake about it." Colonel Christy's pensive face and words suggested he was considering her request.

William exhaled loudly. "If your father is as we suspect—"

"William. Please." Colonel Christy glared at his son then turned his attention to Mercy. "Ignore my son's insinuations. It's my personal belief that Shad fully intended to return here to ask you to marry him."

Mercy's heart hitched a beat. As she, too, had hoped. "What would I have to do to come with you?"

"With us?" William scowled.

"I wouldn't slow you down."

Colonel Christy chuckled. "Always thought you to be a strong woman, Miss Clarke, and if you're anything like William's mother was, you'll do as you wish." Pain skittered across his features.

Was it what God wished, though? She closed her eyes for a moment and prayed. For the first time in weeks, peace cloaked her in comfort.

Fort Detroit

Mercy extended her hands by the wide fireplace that dominated the dining hall, if this ramshackle structure could be called such a thing. Behind her, soldiers jested with one another, and she only shivered more.

"Excuse me, miss." One of the workers, a middle-aged man with a faded blue scarf wound around his neck and attired in heavy wool shirt and pants, motioned for her to move back away from the hearth. When she complied, he added wood and then fanned the fire, stirring up more glowing red charcoals at the bottom.

Since their arrival two days earlier, Mercy's sense of foreboding had been stirred up, like this fire. But it was the ignorance and outright smugness of the officers that chilled her to the bone. They wouldn't listen to the colonel and his son. They'd even had the audacity to toss warning letters from the commander at Fort Pitt into the fire, saying, 'We know our savages here. And we take care of our own.'

A damp breeze accompanied the opening of the door behind her. She turned to see a half-dozen or more men, several of whom were pulling off their reddish knit wool hats. Most were scarcely above her own height, but the confidence and vigor in the few movements they made conveyed strength beneath their loose-fitting coats. All wore deerskins pants, albeit with no decorations or fringe. With their dark hair and eyes and ivory complexions she guessed them to be Frenchmen.

"Hivernauts," a nearby soldier muttered to his companion as he broke a small loaf of bread in half.

Hivernauts? Wasn't that who the colonel was looking for? Or was it voyageurs? Regardless, these might be the men who would accompany them on their trip up Lake Huron. The hivernauts were the men who trapped furs in the winter, but did they also man canoes?

One of the newcomers, a sharp-featured man, with streaks of gray in his hair, scanned the room. His companions eyed the soldiers' tables, which were laid with roast beef, a root vegetable soup, and baskets full of small bread loaves. The serving girl emerged from the kitchen, carrying a tray of what looked like dried apple tarts. She paused when she spied the Frenchmen.

One of the junior officers waved her toward his table. "Feed those men, too, when you're done with us."

She nodded.

The young officer, who had flirted with Mercy the previous night during dinner at the commander's home, stood and approached the group. "Are you here for Christy?" He didn't even address her friend by his rank and Mercy cringed.

"*Oui.*" The lead man spoke for the group.

The officer smirked. "You're welcome to eat here once my men have been fed."

"*Merci.*"

When the lieutenant gestured to their heads, those who hadn't removed their hats did so.

"*Ou est. . .* Where is Christy?"

"He's with the commander." He turned and slapped the back of a nearby private's head. "Take this man to Christy."

"Yes, sir."

Again, Mercy shivered but she turned back to face the fire. The sooner they were out of this place the better. How could Shad have ever thought that she might wish to live here? The women who worked at the fort were very busy and the two she'd spoken with were well-paid. They'd married within weeks of their arrival, too. But Mercy couldn't shake her unease.

Several heavy steps announced movement in her direction. She turned just as the lieutenant extended his hand and grasped her arm. <u>Hard.</u> She shook it and he slackened his grip, but only slightly.

"I really must insist you stay behind with us, Miss Clarke. It's not safe for a woman to undertake such a hazardous journey—especially with these Papist Frenchmen along. Surely you as a minister's daughter don't want to risk this fool-hardy trip."

Once again, she tried to pull away. He leaned in so closely that she could smell the sour ale on his breath. "I can be very persuasive in keeping you here, you know."

The notion of a trip, in a huge canoe, huddled under furs and in the presence of strange Frenchmen suddenly didn't seem as frightening as the alternative.

Chapter 2

Near St. Ignace, early May 1763

Shadrach Clark strained to open his eyes, to no avail, as a Chippewa song, an ancient Algonquin poem celebrating the morning sunrise, pierced his consciousness. How long had he walked this murky road? From path-to-Indian-path to white man's wagon wheel-rutted road, Shad pushed on, staggering—pushing aside mists. All the trails began to look the same and led him to nowhere. Nothing. Only empty space.

Then his wife, Little Fawn, danced toward him and extended her hand. Behind her, the tribal members nodded approvingly, opaque clouds flowing between them and Shad. He batted at the suffocating shroud of mist so he could find his path.

Father, Father, show me the way—I cannot travel this road alone. Heat infused his body as though he were too close to the sun. Above him floated a milky face. Hazel eyes, fringed with long black lashes, searched his unflinchingly.

"We've found you here." A woman. A beautiful English lady. God sent an angel of mercy.

"Please live," she whispered and then pressed the softest lips, like rose petals, onto his forehead.

Closing his eyes again he inhaled—cedar, pine, and the scent of lemon soap and flowers emanating from the beauty. Confused, the odors, mingled with deer hide and smoked fish that marked this place as a Chippewa village—his wife's. But Little Fawn was gone.

Shad drifted off into a fitful sleep. Young Mercy Clarke swirled about in the red wool cape he'd bought her in Williamsburg to replace the dreadful earth-colored one she favored. But when she turned around, she glowed in the morning dawn, her face mature, and the years in between of their many visits over her father's table ran through his mind. In the distance, away from them, a slithering darkness awaited, coiled and ready to strike. He fought to stay near the sunrise while three silken strands of mist held him fast.

"Shad, I'm here. Please wake up." Mercy's voice, so clear, seemed nearby. But that couldn't be. Shivers coursed through him and he shook almost uncontrollably.

Opening his eyes, he squinted. Sunlight drifting through the open door-flap touched his old friend's bronze-gold hair, free about her shoulders. He longed to stretch out and brush back her tresses, to feel their silky heft—like he had when he'd last seen her—and to kiss her. Something restrained him. His body lay immobile—he'd been tethered. Someone had bound him in place.

"Mercy…" his voice emerged as a croak. Truly it was she. Mercy Clarke settled her skirts around her as she lowered onto a low stool near the bed. How could this be that she was here? Shad blinked several times but she was there, sure and certain. His beautiful friend

"You're awake." Her gentle voice held awe. She'd come all this way and surely at great danger to herself.

Mercy leaned forward arms outstretched and a torrent of silky hair fell forward, brushing his cheek, releasing the scent of rosewater. He strained upward to stroke the shimmering waterfall of her waves, but instead his arm held fast.

"Water, please." His parched throat needed liquid desperately.

Mercy lifted a cup to his mouth. Delicious cool water slid down his throat, some down the sides of his face and onto his neck and into his unbound hair. He must smell terrible—how long had he lain here? Shad struggled to pull up but something held him fast.

"Who tied me down?" He tried to kick, but he couldn't.

"I did." The man's British-accented voice pinned him with its authority.

Colonel Christy. Though Shad should be glad, ire rose.

"Cut 'em loose, Colonel. Now!"

Cool fingers stroked his brow—Mercy's touch gentle.

"We feared you'd hurt yourself." The colonel stated dryly as he drew closer.

Colonel Christy's solutions to problems had occasionally endangered others. "What's Mercy doin' here, Colonel?"

"Mercy accompanied me."

Mercy. When had God shown Shad any mercy in his life? A dust mote floated past the young woman's pretty face—her even features worked into a knot of confusion. Her entirety cloaked in autumn hues—an acorn-colored skirt, tawny overblouse, and yellow-gold apron—all disguised her as an oak leaf. He peered down at her feet, expecting brown boots, instead sighting elaborately beaded cream-colored moccasins. He ceased his perusal. He had no business examining a woman who was someone's intended bride. Those heavily beaded shoes marked her as chosen. But for whom? A cold chill ran through his body.

Colonel Christy moved between Shad and Mercy. "I don't know if we should release him yet."

Mercy pushed forward. "Why? He's so sick, colonel, why must they tie him down?"

Shad flexed his arm, a flimsy willow branch, his muscles weak from his prolonged illness.

"Because he broke one of the brave's nose and attacked

31

another during his fever."

She gasped. "He didn't. . ."

"He did indeed. The chief said he fought like a black bear and he could claim a new name were it not for the illness causing his combativeness."

William moved closer and crossed his arms. "I believe it—Shad's a great warrior if need be."

Sweat trickled down Shad's cheek. Weak, so exhausted, and desperate for release, he couldn't speak.

"Please let him go." The young woman's surprisingly solid form slid next to him on the other side of the pallet as she untied his arm. She placed one hand atop Shad's wrist. "You won't hurt me, will you? I'm your friend."

"No, I…" He wanted to hold her hands, to feel some tenderness.

"It's all right, Colonel.

The man's low chuckle accompanied deft fingers as he unfastened the leather ties anchoring Shad to the frame.

She pressed a mug to his lips and he drank the sweet spring water.

When she lay down the mug, he pushed upward and rubbed his freed wrists. "Where'd you get those?" He gestured to the moccasins. Shad gritted his teeth, awaiting her response.

Mercy nodded toward Colonel Christy.

The man flipped his silver queue over one red-coated shoulder. "Rosa said Mercy might need them."

Shad relaxed back into his pine-needle-stuffed pillow, not sure why relief accompanied Colonel Christy's words. Then he remembered. Though he'd said he'd never marry again after losing Little Fawn, he'd given Mercy a tentative promise, or at least he thought he had. His head ached. The last few months were only a hazy blur.

William Christy loomed over him, dark whisker's dotting his cheeks. "Shad?"

"Hmm?" He shook himself, trying to remain alert, but sleep summoned him loudly.

"We need you my friend." The other scout's voice quavered with emotion.

The young woman, lips parted, leaned further in, her arm pressed against his chest, separating her body from his. "You must fight—"

He was a scout, not a soldier. Granted, he'd been involved in more skirmishes than he'd ever planned on. "Fight?"

"For your life, Shad." The way she spoke his name, drawing it out, long and low, caressed his soul, coaxed something within him. She held his arm and began to rub ointment into his chafed wrist.

His hands, freed, twitched—itching to hold hers, wrap around those dainty fingers.

I'll sit with him. You go now."

Weariness weighed Shad down again, taking him to that dark place. Now, though, he fought back against the curtain of cobwebs that called him to a far-off place where he knew he mustn't go. Not yet. When he opened his eyes, again, he spied Mercy reclined on a pallet on the floor, watching him.

"You're really here." He lifted his head from the pillow. "I cannot believe my eyes."

"I am truly here." She sat up and grabbed a bowl that was set on his trunk.

He fought the overwhelming desire to close his eyes.

Mercy came to sit beside him and brushed back a lock of hair from his brow. "You must eat." Her fixed smile suggested he best not give her any resistance.

"Not hungry." He pushed the words past his lips.

"You need to get your strength back."

He managed a chuckle. If what Colonel Christy had said was true then he couldn't have lost it completely.

"Don't even think about going back to sleep." She gave him a stern glance as she stirred the bowl of mush with a wooden spoon, her hip pressed against his.

He quirked his eyebrows back at her, in response.

"Sit up so you can swallow without choking."

"Yes, ma'am." He grinned and scooted back, his weak muscles screaming in protest.

She extended a spoonful of maple-scented corn mush toward him. It didn't smell half-bad and he swallowed it, the texture on his tongue causing a strange reaction. How long had it been since he'd had any food? He resisted the urge to spit it out and reached for the water to chase it down.

Mercy dropped the spoon back into the bowl and handed him the water.

He took a drink, helping the solid food to go down. "Thank you."

"You're welcome." Her beautiful face lit with joy.

He wanted to say he was glad she was there. And he was. But he was also concerned for her. "You've come so far. For me?"

Her cheeks grew rosy. "You've always said there is no place more beautiful than the Straits of Mackinac. I had to come see if you've been lying to me all these years."

He did give a full laugh then. "Ah, did I lie?"

"No." She dipped into the bowl and pushed another spoonful at him. "But there are some things here much better to see than those gorgeous blue waters."

Her gaze connected with his and held. So many words

tried to make their way past his tongue, but they couldn't gather strength to make sound.

Mercy fed him and he continued to assist each mouthful with a sip of water. Outside, sounds of birdsong and of the soft cadence of the Chippewa language reminded him that he was alive. And home. But in the back of his mind niggled the reminder that this was no longer his home. Not with Little Fawn gone. He couldn't gather his thoughts, though.

"God has brought you through this, Shad. And I'm very grateful." Mercy's hopeful expression promised him something.

His argument with God over the tragedies he'd suffered might end.

Shad drifted off to sleep, this new place one of comfort, of clouds, and of warm sunshine breaking in to bathe him in the presence of love. The darkness had fled.

Mercy followed three young Chippewa women to the shores of the great lake. They laughed, splashed, and shared their soft soap as they bathed in the frigid water. She'd missed her mother so much. Until now she hadn't realized what following her father and his quest, had meant—how much his own mission had cost her.

The two younger women chattered in their language—so musical, so gentle. One, with a beautiful smile spoke to her in English, "They say you are Colonel Christy's woman."

The beautiful girl dunked beneath the water and came up laughing. She ran to the shore and wrapped a blanket around her shivering shoulders.

Mercy stared. The man was old enough to be her father. Handsome, yes, wealthy, indeed, but such a thought had never crossed her mind. But it had Rosa's. The gypsy woman considered him to be her spouse regardless of what any laws might say.

"He has been…" she wanted to select a word that would convey a relationship they would understand, ". . . chosen by a woman of the woods, in Virginia."

The oldest girl, perhaps ten and six years old, explained to the others. They looked from one to the other, then nodded.

It was May but the water felt barely above freezing. Indeed, the ice had only gone off the great lake recently. Mercy's teeth chattered together so hard she thought she might chip them. Although she suspected the women were attempting to chill her to death, or at the least humiliate her, she found it hard to believe they'd participate themselves if that were true.

"Our chief's wife says you are Shadrach's woman—but if you are he'll have to go. She won't have you here in our village."

So, she'd had an army lieutenant who'd been determined to keep her at Fort Detroit, but they'd managed to leave early and foil his plans and now because of her they'd have to move on before Shad was ready. Why had she come? But she knew why—a life without Shad in it would be no life at all. Yes, she believed that God had convicted her spirit to make this journey, but she couldn't continue to endanger them all.

After Shad stripped out of his buckskins, William shoved a bundle at him. "Don my shirt and breeches."

Shad shrugged and threw them back on his pallet. But William pushed them into his hands.

"You can't go into the lake with no clothes on."

"Why not? I've been out in colder weather." Shad narrowed his eyes to peer out a gap in the flap, where the sun shone down on the spring day.

Lee Christy's chuckle and crooked grin accompanied his movement as he pulled the flap completely closed and crossed to retrieve the pants. He bent beside Shad's bed and placed William's trousers under Shad's feet.

"I believe you've forgotten that Mercy is in camp."

William snorted and pulled the loaned shirt over Shad's head. "Mercy insisted on taking a bath today, herself."

Slacking his hip, the colonel assumed a bored attitude. "Three long days this young woman has sat beside you as you passed in and out of sleep. Now some of the women assist her in her bathing."

"Then she should be inside of my mother-in-law's lodge enjoying both heated water and soap."

Father and son exchanged a glance. William shook his head. "I saw them heading toward the lake."

"What?" An image of Mercy washing in the lake flooded Shad with more emotions than he realized he had left—warring emotions of anger toward the tribe at subjecting her to the lake and shameful curiosity at the notion of viewing her feminine form in the water. A smile tugged at his lips as his masculine thoughts won out. He wasn't as hopeless as he'd been after his brush with death. Not since Mercy had found him in this village and had ministered to him and his needs. He was alive, well and truly. He drew in a slow and satisfying breath.

The colonel's gray eyes caught his. "She'll likewise be attired, so don't be getting any notions of what you might see out there."

Colonel Christy laughed as he and William pulled Shad up to his feet. He staggered, as the room spun. Closing his eyes, his world slowly straightened out again. Supported between the two Christy men, he emerged through the flap door, the sunlight beating at his eyes. He forced his eyes to open to view the brilliant azure sky. Overhead, robins flitted in and out of the pine trees, returned from their wintering season in the south. The three men meandered toward the great lake, its cerulean beauty belying its cold depths.

Colonel Christy tilted his head, his long silver queue draping his shoulder, "Shall we, gentlemen?"

He kicked off his moccasins as did William. The two men bent to assist Shad with his footwear. With a borrowed pair of William's English-style pant legs unbuttoned and pulled above his knees, Shadrach waded out into the lake water, between the two men. He'd lost so much weight while ill that Shad now fit into his friend's slim pants.

William's strong hand clasped beneath Shad's arm as he took unsteady steps forward. A thousand pinpricks of pain, driven by the cold water, awaited him.

"The quicker we do this, the better."

With that urging, the younger man splashed along with him forward to thigh deep water then released him. Shad gasped as he sank to his knees and he jerked at the colonel's hand.

Lee Christy's dry laugh soothed his terror. "Shad—I do believe you'd drown me just to be contrary, wouldn't you?"

The man knew him well. A chuckle bubbled up through Shad's violent shudders and with it his voice. "If I were a fit man, I'd flip you and dunk you so fast…" There wasn't the strength left in him to accomplish such a feat, but Shad relished the notion that he could.

"'Tis the first step, son—imagining that you could outmaneuver me." The colonel's words rang true.

"I think not, Shad." William's tone irritated the stuffing out of him. "Father isn't called 'Badger' for nothing, you know."

When he was well again, Shad would teach his younger friend a thing or two. He would rearrange William's bad attitudes till they lined up right again. Why must he and William be at odds with each other again so soon—like two brothers vying for a father's attention? With William now five and twenty, couldn't they let this struggle go?

"First few moments in the water are frightful cold." Colonel Christy's comment seemed directed to no one in particular.

With a shudder, Shad tried to move his legs. "Then my body goes numb? You believe that fever sapped what little intelligence I had?"

Christy chuckled. "Actually—I was warning William, not you. I imagine that you're quite familiar with the sensation of this frigid water, are you not?"

A loon called to its mate and Shad shivered. The cry went unanswered. The loons had begun to return. Where had they been? He'd never seen one in the western reaches of Virginia when he'd lived there. The loon repeated its lonesome call. No answer.

Collapsing into the icy-cold water, Shad held his breath. If there was any fever left in him, 'twould be frozen out now. He raised his head above the water and William shoved soap at him. As quickly as he could, Shad worked it into his hair, his teeth chattering. He'd strip out of William's clothes after and let the women wash them and hang them to dry near the fires.

Shad extended his legs and floated for a moment, forcing himself to endure the cold. *Might as well die from freezing as anything else. But Lord, I want to live.*

Shad's heartbeat slowed as he submerged beneath the still surface of the frigid lake. He floated, suspended in the waves. His pulse returned with vigor. This was real. He was alive. He groped for Christy's hands and pulled up. He shook his head hard, knew it would spray onto William and enrage him. As soon as the younger man groaned, Shad turned. He'd wash away his cocky attitude. William gasped as Shad pushed him under. 'Twas awful good to be alive. Awful good.

Shad laughed as William sputtered and rose up, shaking his head and fists—safer he didn't have a knife on him.

Lee Christy's clear gray eyes met Shad's. "Shall I raise you up?"

Chills, having nothing to do with the water, chased down Shad's chest. Christy's question had to do with getting him to stand and nothing to do with salvation. But the man's question was one his father, a preacher, liked to ask his parishioners. Pa, with a flair for the dramatic, would don a simple robe and throw his arms wide, asking if anyone in the congregation wanted to be baptized. *And then be "raised up."*

Where was Reverend John Clark now? Shad's teeth chattered. He nodded and Christy hauled him upward. His trembling legs found footing and the man released him.

Christy gestured toward shore, where the young woman stood shivering. "Mercy chose to come with us. Insisted— said her spirit was disturbed when she heard of your plight. And we still don't know where Reverend Clarke is."

Only God knew where both of their fathers were. He tensed as the cool water swirled around him, trying to visualize his sister, Rachel, in his mind. She'd be Mercy's age now. William's wet hands gripped viselike as he dragged Shad forward.

"I thank God the natives on Mackinac Island could tell us where to find you. Because now I can help you get well so I can…" William's veiled threat was accompanied by a laugh.

What--prove that William was a man to be reckoned with? A scout as notable as himself? The burst of energy Shad had experienced in pulling William down with him vanished. With it came the remorse of his actions—childish, irrational behavior. Hadn't he become a man? A good husband to his wife—responsible and true? She'd been gone now for a year. If she were looking down from heaven she would frown on his behavior. And she'd also tell him to go on with his life. To find another wife.

Little Fawn loved traveling to the Great Island, Mackinac, the Great Turtle, situated halfway between St. Ignace and what had been the French fort on the other side of the water. They'd remain there several days, at their cabin in the center of the island, before joining the others at Fort Michilimackinac on the mainland when the voyageurs came in. Shad's wife excelled at haggling with the French merchants there to get the best price on goods. She'd loved to attend the autumn maple syrup festival. But then some angry Huron took Little Fawn's life. They said in retaliation for the English victory—that Shadrach might be untouchable at the fires but the fires were now gone out with the English in control.

"You shouldn't blame yourself for what the Huron did to Little Fawn."

Was William now reading his mind?

His friend stared at the clear water. "They didn't kill her because of you. You might be a great scout for the British, but…"

"Former scout," he growled.

Lee Christy's jaw muscle twitched. "The Huron simply attacked the Chippewa in an attempt to control the island. Little Fawn was not the only one killed. And as you know, they are gone now."

They continued toward the beach and finally Shad's feet connected with cold dry earth. "You shouldn't have brought Mercy here."

His mother-in-law stood not a stone's throw away. Called Nokomis or grandmother, for the number of her grandchildren was great, she displayed no affection as she affixed agate-cold eyes upon him. With her arms braced across her chest, Shad was reminded of the woman's stance and accompanying accusation years earlier—'Why can't you give Little Fawn children? She will need a warrior for a husband, not an Englishman who runs through the forests.' Nokomis had spat on the cedar strewn ground then and looked as though she wished to do the same now. And he had no doubt that she wished him gone from her sight.

If the reports were true, if the Chippewa of Michilimackinac sought to rise up in protest against the English, would Nokomis convince the chief to go along with them? Prickles of warning raced up his neck, like players battling in a game of baggataway.

Chapter 3

The cold water had revived not only Shad's spirits but his appetite as well. He sat in the circle with the others, eating their meal.

William's nostrils narrowed, as though he smelled something bad. "Doesn't taste as good as Sarah's cooking." His wife Sarah could do no wrong—at least according to William.

Shad slowly chewed the deer meat stew. This wasn't as delicious as Mercy's meals—the last served to Shad over two months earlier. He closed his eyes for a moment, remembering the savory broths she'd prepared for her roasts. More than the food, he'd relished her kiss on that visit, as well and wished to repeat it, but well away from this encampment.

Lee Christy set down his own unfinished and half-filled wooden platter on the ground, earning him a scathing look from the chief's wife, from across the fire. Nokomis hated to waste food and Christy's failure to consume all implied their victuals were lacking. "Agreed, son. My daughter-in-law is a fine cook. But 'tis time you brought her and the boys to Philadelphia and let our cook there take that chore from her."

William grunted—whether in agreement or disagreement it wasn't clear.

Shad reached down and speared the remains of the venison from the colonel's supper. Then he finished off William's, too, plus his own food, and then stacked the three platters. Nokomis actually smiled and nodded at him from where she sat with the women.

Leaning toward his friend, he couldn't resist a tease. "Watch out, William. Soon you'll be a city gent and Sarah and the boys will take up the gentrified life you've denied yourself during the war."

"She loves those Blue Ridge Mountains. Wants to be near her family."

Venison stuck in Shad's throat. "I have family somewhere."

Colonel Christy chuckled. 'Twas good that Mercy and her father hadn't been your family, after all."

"I didn't mean to stir sad memories." William's black eyes flashed sympathy.

"My sister Rachel must be married, with children, by now." As Mercy should be. Which he may never be able to give her since he and Little Fawn had never had any of their own.

Colonel Christy moved to a seat on a low stump. "Colonel McCready is exploring all avenues in search of your family, Shad, now that the infernal war is over. He's instructed all officers to inform me if they have word of your family. Including those in the areas we've taken in the far north."

"Thank you. But I am no longer a scout in His majesty's service and they owe me nothing."

"A highly renowned scout." Christy's gentle smile and nod bathed Shad in approval. "And we owe you much."

Mercy's admiring hazel eyes caught his and he averted his gaze. "My parents…"

The words tripped from his lips like a prayer. Ones he'd beseeched God with over and over again when he feared for his life in the Shenandoah Valley, begging God to bring them to rescue him from the brutal man who'd married his aunt and dragged them to the wilderness. God rest his aunt's soul. Yet hadn't God used that time, and Shad's rescue, to mold him into who he'd become? But what was he? A man without much to his name. Yet there was the cabin on Mackinac. They could go there.

Nokomis narrowed her eyes at him. The women's mood could shift like the breeze that tickled the tops of the pines. Now that he was well, Shad would leave this village.

"Let's head to the Great Turtle soon." What would it be like to have Mercy there on the beautiful island with him? He flushed with the notion of her being with him in the cabin for the night. He'd not leave her with his mother-in-law and the other women who'd begun to shun her. But with Christy and William accompanying them, all should be well. Unless the rumors about Fort Michilimackinac being at risk of attack were true.

Mercy ducked her head and entered Shad's dwelling. With the airing they'd given it earlier, and with his bath and the washing of clothes, the smell inside was much more pleasant. Nokomis had also sent cedar incense that after burning left behind a lingering spicy scent. With Shad now in better health, she shouldn't sleep there alone with him. The colonel and his son had slumbered in the great lodge and taken turns caring for Shad. But she doubted their welcome would continue for long. She rubbed her arms, beneath the thin striped wool blanket she'd been given by Nokomis's eldest daughter when they took Mercy's cloak to wash and dry. The doeskin gown she wore was butter-soft but she'd never slept in such a garment. She turned—she should go out and ask to sleep with one of the families. Yet who would have her?

She was just about to lift the flap, when William entered, stepping onto her foot.

"Ow!" She lifted her offended foot.

"Sorry, Mercy." William chewed his lower lip. "We

need to move in here with you and Shad."

Wrapping his hand around her shoulder, William moved Mercy aside as his father and Shad pushed through the entrance, carrying wooden cots.

"Excuse us." Colonel Christy passed her and moved toward the stack of furs on the floor. "We felt it was best to join you."

Had Nokomis disinvited them from her lodge? Mercy's mouth went dry.

In the dim light of the bear grease lamp, the three men set up the cots and hoisted the bedcoverings atop. They pushed one makeshift bed further away from Shad's large pallet. Presumably for her.

The colonel sat down and removed his boots. William arranged his weapons beside his bed. Fear clawed at her insides. Surely they were safe here, in the village Shad had belonged to for so many years.

"Best catch some shut eye, Mercy." Shad's firm tone held an edge.

Now hours later, Mercy still couldn't fall into slumber. Mercy's emotions roiled within her like the ship from England had done years earlier, over the vast Atlantic Ocean. The hut's bark walls closed in on her and urged her feet to take her to a place where she could be alone.

William's gentle breathing and the colonel's periodic snorts assured her they slept, so Mercy pulled the wool blanket from the top of her coverings and wrapped herself in it. She slipped her feet into the elaborate moccasins and departed as quietly as she could.

Once outside, the brilliant early May moon shone down on the village. Beyond the jagged dark pines that lined the beach, lay the glistening water—black with silvery movement in its waves. She inhaled the scent of deer meat and corn and the whiff of fresh green growth. She moved toward the water, but the chill of the spring night and her flimsy foot coverings soon left her shivering.

What was she doing here? She'd made herself ridiculous coming after Shad. Moisture pooled in her eyes then spilled down her cold cheeks. She wiped them away. *God, what have I done?*

Behind her, heavy footfall scraped across the sandy soil. She turned, unsure who to expect.

Moonlight illuminated Shad's face and glistened his blond hair. "What are you doing out here, Mercy girl?"

"I…"

"Can't you sleep? Aren't you used to the Christy men and their snoring by now?" His low laugh made her smile. He moved closer to her.

"The colonel has a manner of sounds, doesn't he?" She pulled the blanket tighter.

"Still a might cold out here for moonlight walks. Are you looking for the spirits of the two lovers?" His voice held a tease.

"Who?"

Shad took her hand, his fingers warm as he pulled her toward a massive white rock nearby. He motioned for her to sit atop its flat surface and she did. When he sat beside her, she tried to scoot over, but his hip pinned her blanket.

He wrapped an arm around her. "I'll keep you warm while I tell you the story, but then you must come back inside and sleep."

Although he'd not brought another Hudson Bay blanket with him, Shad's body heat warmed Mercy down to her chilly toes. "Tell me the legend."

"Well, first of all, you need to know that the lovers won't be found here at all." He rested his head atop hers.

"They won't?" Mercy's breathless voice sounded as though it belonged to someone else. She could hear her heartbeat in her ears as she leaned against Shad's chest inhaling the lemon soap he'd bathed with earlier.

"No. You'll only see them on Mackinac Island. Which is why I shall save this story and take you there very soon."

She pulled away from him. "You've piqued my interest, and now you shan't tell me? You wicked man!"

Taking her hand, he raised it to his lips and pressed a kiss into her palm. "All in good time. But for now, I say we get you to sleep and rested. For tomorrow I begin my recovery in earnest. And I shall require your good services as nurse."

"Yes, of course." She drew in a deep breath. "We'll have you walk the trail they say leads to St. Ignace. 'Tis well-marked and steady, they say."

He laughed. "As you wish. Come now—rest."

Shad stood and pulled her to her feet. And back to his shelter.

The "dipping" by the colonel and his son, infused Shad's recovery. His strength hastened so rapidly that he and several of the braves had traveled to Naubinway by foot and back that next day. Christy stayed behind, but William had joined them, asking questions of all they encountered.

"Have you seen the English soldiers here? Have they sent you messengers from Michilimackinac?" Most replied that they hadn't, but their wary looks put Shad on edge.

When they returned, Nokomis surprised him by sending a request that he assist in gathering and hauling wood for the fires on the following day. "She said it will strengthen your arms," Little Fawn's sister informed him. But she seemed to be holding back a giggle at the notion of him performing women's work.

Now tonight he'd enjoy the smoked fish they'd brought back with them, yesterday, from the former French outpost near Naubinway. Since the French-Indian War had ended, many of the Métis fishing families had dispersed further into the forest, not wishing to bring attention to themselves. But few had actually left the area, despite it now being owned by the British.

Mercy scuffled across the yard, toward him, still wearing the infernal wedding moccasins she'd been given. He'd need to do something about them soon for they'd provide little protection on the hilly terrain of the island.

When she reached him, she touched his wrist, just below his deerskin sleeve, sending a powerful wave of warmth through him. He resisted the urge to pull her into his arms and kiss her right there in front of everyone. But it wouldn't be proper and they'd not yet come to an understanding.

Her cheeks reddened, as though she'd read his thoughts. "Your fish is being served now."

"Is that so?"

"Yes." She laughed and then pulled him toward the circle that ringed the cooking pit. The other women scurried around the fire, but as they joined the group, they didn't encourage Mercy to assist.

When Nokomis shot them a stern look, Mercy released his arm. "They told me to sit with you."

He gestured toward the spot where William and Lee Christy were settling themselves. They joined the two and Shad held Mercy's hand as she lowered herself onto a blanket beside William.

"Thank you, Shad." Firelight flickered in Mercy's warm eyes. What would it be like to look at those inviting eyes every night? Every day?

After they'd eaten the delicious white fish, rose, pleased his legs could easily support him again.

Flames flickered in Williams' eyes, his face as placid as the *Lac du Michigan* waters nearby. "You have your strength back." His clipped intonation sent a message that he had far more he meant to say.

"I do. Hauling wood for the women helped, even as embarrassing as that was."

William tossed a stick into the fire. "We've waited until you were well to warn you." He inclined his head toward his father.

So that was it. They were finally going to tell him what was going on that they would search him out so diligently. "Warn me about what?"

Colonel Christy stood and stretched. The man *did* resemble a badger, and heaven help the man who resisted him— he'd be torn apart.

"What troubles have you had here before you fell ill, before the changeover even from French to British control?"

Shad looked from father to son. William tossed one broken stick after another into the flames.

"Before the English took over the fort, it was peaceful here. The French and Ojibway had good relations. They understood and respected one another."

"Yet it is not so now." Christy rubbed his forefinger along the bridge of his aristocratic nose.

William spat into the dirt. "We should get you out of here soon."

Shad's knees stiffened. He forced himself upright. "What do you mean?"

The rustling Northern pines whispered dark low secrets.

"There is unrest. The British are not responding to the

tribes' requests. We need to discover more about how we can keep the peace."

William's black eyebrows pulled together. "Or if, as I believe, peace is <u>not</u> an option."

If the Ojibway, Ottawa, and Pottawatomi tribal confederation could not reach a satisfactory resolution with the English, Shad could not stay either.

"I doubt any Englishman would be safe here. But I pray you are wrong."

Pray. When had he last prayed? When Mercy had come to him.

Shad swiveled toward Mercy. Something in his life had to give way. Scouting had caught up to him and hammered him to the ground. Broke him. Yet the Lord had sent this angel. Mercy. To find him. To welcome him back home to Christ. Christy's immersion of Shad in the lake water had done more than relieved him of the stench that had clung to him. Rather it also woke his resolve to be clean in God's sight, too. And that decision, while it had continued, hadn't been followed by submitting his own will to the Lord's.

Mercy's lips parted as Shad held out his hand for her. He pulled her to standing, aware that on the other side of the fire, Little Fawn's parents watched.

The colonel wandered off in the chief's direction, but William remained behind, watching his father.

Shad gazed into the eyes of the woman he yearned to have as his wife. Who'd rescued him from death. She with these two men and the Lord.

His heart needed a home—one with her in it. Yet he had nothing to offer her. Not if the English, including himself, needed to abandon this area.

As he leaned in toward her, his shoulder pressed against Mercy's. He'd not move away from her though—would let her move back if she wished. But she remained where she was, albeit with her eyes turned away from his. Breathing deeply, he drew in the scent of fir and the subtle scent of flowers and soap that belonged uniquely to her.

"We can't stay with this tribe anymore, you know. I'll have to leave." Shad looked across the fire at his mother-in-law, whose eyes flickered back and forth between him and Mercy. "They are calling you my woman."

Mercy's gasp of outrage was accompanied by an elbow to his rib and he leaned away from her as she turned toward him. "I never made any such claim!"

He raised his hands. "Never said you did."

Happiness grew in him at the notion that the women in camp had noticed feelings that they'd not yet expressed to one another. He bowed his head, his hair brushing against the side of his face, shielding his smile from his beloved.

"No." Mercy turned and leaned forward as though she could discern from a glance across the fire what the other women's thoughts were.

Lips thinning, Nokomis looked as though she'd found something distinctly bitter in her drink.

Returning his attention to Mercy, Shad whispered into her ear, "We'll go to Mackinac, to the island, and take up residence in my cabin."

She jerked away from him. "Excuse me, but I'll not be living with you, unmarried, anywhere."

He froze, tempted to grab her hand but now catching the dark gaze of his father-in-law. "Christy and William will accompany us and we'll all stay there until I figure out…"

Figure out what to do with the rest of his life? He gazed out at the pink-tinged water, the slowly setting sun hanging over the azure waters. God knew he'd seen enough fighting, enough sorrow, enough hurt in his life. All he wanted now was comfort. And Mercy. But how would he provide for them? He had winter furs to exchange, but not in sufficient number to set up household again, should he have to leave the island behind. He rubbed a spot between his eyebrows, praying for wisdom.

"I see." Her words, barely audible. "We'd need to leave soon then. But you aren't ready to make your next decision, is my assumption."

So, Shad still hadn't decided if he'd marry her. Mercy struggled to keep her emotions in check. She balled her fists. She'd traveled this long distance through dangerous climes yet he couldn't decide?

"Mercy, I don't think I want to…"

William grabbed at Shad's shoulder. "Come on—let's practice our baggataway skills."

The game, much like the French sport of Lacrosse was said to be a skill-honing practice for battle.

Shad's mouth dropped open and he frowned as though to protest but then said nothing.

"I haven't had a chance in a long time," William persisted.

"Maybe I can." Shad glanced across the fire again as though some cue from the colonel was guiding his behavior.

Christy nodded and Shad rose. The two younger men headed off to a nearby clearing where they were joined by some of the other braves, all laughing.

Mercy scrubbed her wood plate with sand and returned it to the stack. The young woman motioned her away and scowled. Although initially welcoming, they'd turned sullen since discovering she was Shad's friend, construed as 'his woman'.

Despite the flush of heat in her cheeks, she pulled her cloak around her, against the light breeze that whispered through the pines. Shad and William played what the French called lacrosse with the young men. She couldn't help smiling—Shad's agility increased rapidly. He was recovering well. The men's hoots and hollers were so loud, she wondered how they concentrated upon their game.

Throughout the village, all had a task, save she—other than helping clean Shad's dwelling. With a shake of her shoulders she headed toward the water, movement far off from shore catching her attention. As she raised her hand to her eyes, she caught the glint of metal from a long boat, filled with native men. Their hair struck her as especially odd—as thought they were partially bald, but on the sides of their heads. Her hand flew to her mouth as sun glistened the blue-black hair of the men's top knots.

Warriors rowed toward them, their faces painted fearsomely. She stood, unable to move, her mouth open like the trout in the rivers nearby. Breech cloths covered their middles, but their thighs were bare, despite the cool air.

She gasped.

Movement from behind and footfall of the men caused her to turn. Shad's light eyes caught hers in the field of dark gazes as all looked toward the newcomers.

"Chequamegon!" one of the braves nearby announced.

Shad grabbed her hand. "We must hide you, Mercy."

Perspiration glistened on his forehead.

"A war party?"

"They are not our allies." The tremor in his voice sent shards of fear up her spine.

One of the younger men ran to the chief as Shad clasped her hand and yanked her toward his dwelling. "None of the tribes have accepted the decision made by the French and English kings."

The women emerged from the longhouse and those working outside moved toward the shoreline.

Lee and William Christy ran up behind them, startling Mercy. She clung to Shad's hand, his arm brushing hers as they ducked inside his shelter.

"The Anishinaabe are a peace-loving people in general. They accept the arrival of the British and do not wish to become involved in any conflict. But others stir up strife."

Dear Lord, help us. Were the rumors true that an attack on the English was planned and even imminent?

Colonel Christy squared his shoulders. "'Tis the Chequamegon and their leader and I've need to speak with them." Although his voice was strong, Mercy heard the slight quiver in his words. "We were sent here to gauge what the tribes think about the English proposition of withholding gifts and giving only to those deemed supportive of the King's agenda."

The British officer's curt comments conflicted with what she'd heard him say—that the wrong-minded philosophy would backfire. Or had it already gone awry—with no recovery? And possibly their deaths at the hands of these heathens painted for war?

Chapter 4

They all entered the birch bark hut, one after the other. Mercy's heart pounded so hard that she heard it beating in her ears. She stood to the side, clutching her hands.

"I will not hide in here like a coward." Colonel Christy paced back and forth beneath the dome-like roof. "They will speak to me as Badger."

The officer's Shawnee name was Badger, given by his former father-in-law, a chief in one of the Iroquois tribes. A fierce fighter, Christy was well-respected. But what was one man against so many if they had come to attack?

Dressed in buckskins and moccasins, the colonel didn't resemble the red-coated officer who'd often visited Mercy's home.

William grabbed his father's sleeve. "I'll accompany you."

Shad had sunk to the bed, sweat drenching his brow. "Mercy, get behind me, under the covers. Just in case something goes wrong."

There was no escape if the colonel and his son were attacked. Killed. Shad slid a hatchet and three knives beneath the blanket.

The colonel motioned her to the raised pallet. "Do as he says."

Mercy legs shook as she climbed across the furs, behind Shad, and then slid beneath them, their weight heavy. Her foot brushed against his firm calf and she flinched.

"This is improper," she whispered into his golden hair. Yet she recognized the absurdity in her words.

"Better chance for you to live if they've come to kill."

Uncontrollable tremors shook through Shad's body,

recalling the terror he'd experienced long ago when renegade Shawnee attacked his Virginia cabin. Unlike those many years earlier, he would not abandon Mercy as he'd left his aunt. Instead of his current eight and twenty years, he fleetingly experienced the terror of the twelve-year-old he'd been. The boy who'd warned his abusive uncle that rebel Shawnee intended to attack their home in the Shenandoah Valley. Only to be rewarded with a swift backhand that had sent Shad to his knees.

When William, then a young boy living with his grandfather's tribe, had returned to Shad, to help him escape, Shad had no choice but to leave his aunt and uncle behind. They wouldn't listen. How many times had Shad replayed the horrific scene in his mind?

He'd not leave Mercy. He'd die before one of them touched her. His final act on earth would be spent defending the woman he loved.

Mercy pressed a hand to his shoulder. "We should pray."

"Yes." His croak sounded more like the boy he'd been. He cleared his throat. Peace, unbidden, unasked for, coursed like the great nearby falls of Tahquamenon through him.

"All shall be well." That promise tripped from his lips as though he knew. But he didn't. One greater than them knew, though—and he'd have to trust God.

As the sun rose the following day, Colonel Christy grasped Mercy's elbow and guided her toward the awaiting birch canoe. "The Chequamegon may have been placated for now but I fear once we are gone they shall return and press their case."

William, his face reflecting a ferocity Mercy had never

seen, leaned in and hissed, "We go now, while they yet sleep."

Shad shot his friend a quick glance before he assisted Mercy into the boat.

Soon they were underway, moving further from the shoreline. Shad's shoulders moved in perfect rhythm as he dipped his oars from one side to the other of the birch canoe as he took her away, moving past the village and away from the tiny fishing settlement of Epoufette.

"You've made an excellent recovery," Colonel Christy called above the splash of the oars and the lilting breeze.

Shad called back over his shoulder, "Good day for this trip, Colonel."

He made it sound as though they'd not had to depart under possible threat of losing their lives. Maybe that's how Shad had lasted as a scout so long – by making light of his circumstances. Seated in the middle between the men, Mercy sat still as the men dipped their paddles into and out of the water in deft rhythm.

The colonel paused. "We'll take you to the large island we passed en route here."

"Situated in the straits?" They'd pointed out the rough area as they'd passed on their initial voyage north.

"Yes."

Mackinac Island lay where two large inland bodies of water as large as seas, *lacs* the French called them, or lakes, came together. Cerulean blue and shades of indigo she'd never seen varied the waterway as they continued on. "It's much prettier today than when we passed through earlier. And as beautiful as Shad had promised me all these years."

"The sun's out." Christy raised his voice above the splash of the water and resumed his work.

Wrapped in a fur cloak, Mercy pulled her wool scarf to

cover her cheeks. Shad's recovery seemed miraculous—truly heaven sent. Less than a week earlier he lay near death, and now his agile movements evidenced strength, and determination. But if the Chequamegon wished to attack the British, as the colonel and his son suspected, then why would they be spared? She shivered despite her warm clothes.

Shad glanced at her face and his features grew tense. "Mercy, I plan to show you my home and I pray you will be comfortable there."

What did that mean? She shifted, but only a little, not wanting to rock their vessel. The island, impossibly verdant for so early spring, was covered in lush pine and cedar—it looked like a large emerald lying in a field of sapphires. From the distance, she spied sandy shores.

As though reading her mind, Shad called back, "Don't forget the rocky bottom as we near."

Soon they pulled close to the northwestern side of Mackinac. A very faint scent of woodsmoke portended that someone cooked nearby on the island.

"My Chippewa brothers tell me the Huron have left—this time we hope for good." Shad disembarked first, hip deep in the water. He looked like he was trying hard not to shiver in the cold water.

He pulled the canoe near a wide swath of beach. William handed down supplies to Shad and then got out. Christy did the same, leaving Mercy in the canoe. Shad pulled the canoe onward as Christy and son took the supplies back and waded toward the shore.

Looking into the canoe at her, Shad grinned, his face already dotted with red-gold stubble despite the sun being full overhead. If he were an Amish man, he'd not have to bother with scraping his face.

"Don't worry, I won't let you drown." He laughed then splashed a palm full of sparkling water at her.

Mercy threw her hands up, as the icy water assailed her. Before she knew what had happened, Shad had grabbed her hands, pulled her across his shoulders like a bag of grain, and was carrying her toward the shore with her body pressed indecently against his back—the colonel and his son laughing. She tried to beat at his chest, but the heavy furs prohibited movement.

"Oh, hush now, Mercy, I mean you no harm." Shad's soothing voice held a tease. "Just knew you would hesitate was all, and I didn't want you getting flustered and falling in the water."

"Flustered?" Flustered. She'd show Shadrach Clark what flustered looked like. She was reminded of the lady's man he'd been before he'd married Little Fawn. Always rushing to help damsels in distress—often to be sent scurrying by their beloveds. Well she had no one to chase him off. Not unless God counted. And He seemed to have thrown them together rather than separated them. Her heart was a dulcimer that Shad's steps hammered upon as he carried her forward to what she prayed would be a safe place. Away from the visiting Chequamegon at least.

"Bonjour!" A man's voice rang out nearby. Mercy sucked in a breath. Shad bent and set her on the new spring grass her feet groping to find her footing.

Shad wiped his hands.

"Father Menard, what are you doing here?" Shad swiped at his forehead.

A priest, dress in black robes, partially covered by a fur cloak, stood on a foot path by the woods.

"Where is it I am to go?" His heavily accented English was accompanied by raised hands, as though beseeching heaven for an answer.

Coming alongside her, Shad gripped Mercy's elbow as he called out, "St. Ignace, perhaps?"

"Oui, that I did and learned Pierre, like Angelique, has gone to be with the Lord, our Savior." Father Menard made the sign of the cross.

Under his breath Shad muttered something. His features tugged together in consternation.

She turned to look at the scout. This close, his face mere inches from her own, she took in his handsome features—high cheekbones, his square jaw, and a firm nose pleasing in profile. Did she wish him to be her husband only because of his appearance—no, she'd known him too long to think such an absurd thought.

"I am very sorry to hear this, Father Menard." Shad rubbed at his chin. "And who is caring for the child?"

"I have kept her with me in my little hut. We're with the Chippewa encamped here by the harbor, if you wish to check on her."

Shad nodded slowly.

"She seems quite happy playing with the other children." The priest smiled. "I think she's been lonely for the company *d'autres de son âge*."

Colonel Christy pulled a walking stick from his pack and leaned on it for a moment. "Yes, I imagine she would enjoy being with children her own age."

"Oui." The priest nodded.

"We need to speak with you, Father, about another matter of grave concern." Colonel Christy's brow furrowed. "About Pontiac stirring up trouble. Have there been any braves on the island who follow his path?"

"*Je ne sais quois*. I don't know." The Frenchman flipped his palms upward. "But the little girl, is she not, too, as you say a grave matter? And she has been asking for you, Monsieur Clark."

He pronounced Shad's name like *clerc*, a word meaning cleric or clergyman. The priest raised one dark eyebrow in accusation.

Shad released her elbow and marched toward the priest—not angrily but with determination. Who were Pierre and Angelique?

Mercy strode to where Christy still stood, the breeze causing her skirts to undulate around her.

His silver-gray eyes searched hers. "We've heard of this child before and have spoken with the native people near Fort Michilimackinac. We believe the child was kidnapped before the war ended."

She frowned. "A Métis child?" Heat infused her cheeks—she'd heard from Shad how the French soldiers often had native wives and families with them.

Christy dropped his gaze and dug the toe of his boot into the soft sand, the scents of nearby pines wafting toward them. He met her eyes again, a muscle in his cheek twitching. "No, a little French girl—with eyes bluer than Shad's."

As Shad conversed with the priest, in rapid French, he jabbed his hand at the air, pointing inward toward the center of the island. She rubbed her arms beneath the fur cape.

Christy drew in a long breath and held it before slowly exhaling through puffed out lips. "I am greatly concerned who the girl's true father may be…"

"What do you mean?"

He shook his head slowly. "Someone very important and I pray I am wrong. It could complicate my life if I must set the situation aright, through diplomacy. And I certainly couldn't proceed until I am back in Philadelphia."

"Oh." A very important Frenchman? The French officers from Fort Michilimackinac were gone.

The priest clapped Shad on his shoulder and headed toward a nearby path.

The man she'd grown to love joined her. "Come on. We've got a long walk to the interior where my cabin is." He motioned William and his father to follow them into the woods.

As they moved further into the interior, snow still clung in minuscule mounds beneath the forest canopy. Birds twittered and swooped overhead. Cool gusts of wind stirred the new growth on bushes that flanked the trail. Finally, when her skirt's hem was almost soaked with mud, they entered a clearing ringed in cedars, spruce, and low pines. Ferns of all kinds pushed at the earth and the humusy air promised new growth and spring.

"We'll bring in dry wood." Christy and son headed to the woodpile nearby, covered by an overhang.

The main structure, almost as large as her home in Pennsylvania, was a log cabin that appeared to be at least two rooms deep and two wide. The chimney's height and roofline suggested either a second floor or a sleeping loft.

"What do you think?" Shad's warm hand settled possessively on her cheek, his rough thumb stroking a path across her cheekbone.

He was close—*much too close*—she could feel the heat emanating from his body. Mercy swallowed.

"I . . ." He seemed to be asking her much more than simply her opinion of the structure. "I have to admit I am surprised to see such a substantial structure here."

His features hardened as though she'd affronted him. He looked away from her, toward the south.

Covering his hand with hers, she pulled his fingers from her face. "It's very nice."

"Mercy, there will be more people, soldiers likely, coming here if the fools running the forts in Detroit and Mackinac don't listen to Colonel Christy—and they certainly didn't listen on his way here."

"No, they did not." She'd overheard some of their conversation, mostly about how the natives didn't like the way the English did things and that they must try to get along. But the commanders seemed to dismiss Christy's concerns, even when William vehemently argued their point—and stalked off after both encounters with the men. The commander at Michilimackinac, Captain Etheredge, even threatened William if he ever brought him such news again, calling him a coward. When they'd left Michilimackinac, she stood in her red cloak at the fort's exit and looked out toward the water, wondering about what threats could cross those turbulent waters.

She shivered. "And those Chequamegon?"

"Christy and William both seemed mighty restless to talk to Etheridge again at Michilimackinac and then make a decision."

Shad swallowed, his Adam's apple bobbing. "Hopefully, we'll have at least a fortnight on the island before we must make some decisions."

"Two weeks?" Might she only have a short time on this beautiful island? What if the decision was to leave?

"Maybe less."

Mercy should not be here on the island—so close to Fort Michilimackinac, across the straits. Shad knew it, but oh how he longed to finally make her his wife—if she agreed.

Over dinner that night, venison stew with potatoes and what was left of his rutabagas, he and the Christys spoke about what the commanders had said. The intelligence they'd gathered as they scouted on their way north suggested Pontiac was gathering influence and stirring up trouble against the English—but was he so foolish as to attack?

William hacked at his vegetables with a sharp knife. "The Chequamegon didn't speak freely with our Chippewa brothers in the village—not with us there. I plan to return to them in a few days and inquire."

"We have to make at least one more attempt to warn the commander at Michilimackinac." Christy ate his stew slowly while William tipped back his bowl and drank from it, earning him a scathing look from his father.

"They don't deserve it." William's upper lip curled in disdain.

"Nor do they deserve to be attacked, though." Christy cleared his throat and looked at Mercy.

William swiped at his mouth. "Some people think they know all. They believe they are God."

Mercy's hazel eyes widened but she said nothing, making Shad proud that she wasn't the type of woman to become agitated easily. Her strong faith protected her. He, too, felt God's peace in the midst of their tenuous situation. "The little girl, Jacqueline—could you make inquiries?"

Shad had heard the rumors. "Do you think she could have been the French commander's child?"

"The French King's Commandant, Monsieur Beaujeu de Villemonde, and all his troops left Michilimackinac in the autumn of 1760. He isn't here to speak for himself and his wife. Christy's silver eyes cut to Mercy and back to Shad. "We should be careful about what could be rumors."

Shad reached for a piece of sweet squaw bread that Nokomis had sent. The chief's wife too, had feared that the girl may belong to the former commander of Fort Michilimackinac—now returned to his homeland. Nokomis repeated what she'd heard from a Métis trapper. He said that he believed childless trapper Pierre and his wife Angelique had lost another baby near the time the French fort commander's wife gave birth. And he'd seen the very distressed Pierre at Michilimackinac when the Voyageurs had come in. During the chaos of that initial arrival day, the commander's infant went missing, and was never found. When Shad met Pierre and Angelique, the two claimed that they were Jacqueline's birth parents. They certainly acted as devoted parents. Both Little Fawn and Shad had served as aunt and uncle when they were on Mackinac Island. Pierre was gone trapping on the mainland frequently. Angelique and Pierre kept to themselves even before the English arrived. Many of the Métis families disappeared into the vast northern woods when the English had arrived—farther than any of the small British commands could ever manage to penetrate. But Pierre and Angelique had done the opposite.

"What did the priest say?" The colonel's nostrils flared as though challenging Shad to not answer.

He felt as though he'd swallowed a bag of black powder, his gut felt so heavy.

"Father Menard said he spoke with the priest who'd been at the fort during the end of the French occupation."

"And?" The colonel quirked an eyebrow at Shad.

"He told Father Menard that the missing infant who he'd baptized had wisps of blonde hair and bright sapphire eyes." Shad exhaled sharply. "Like Jacqueline has."

"Pierre and Angelique were as dark as I am." William

placed a hand on his black hair with one hand and aimed two fingers towards his eyes with the other.

Shad stifled a grin. William was speaking with his hands again after being back with the tribe. "Angelique had a miniature of her mother, who had fair hair and light eyes." Or was the tiny portrait truly of her mother?

Mercy's eyebrows raised. "So where are the commander and his family now?"

Colonel Christy cocked his head. "Geneviève Beaujeu de Villemonde was the daughter of a wealthy landowner and former Governor of Trois-Rivières. But it's believed that they returned to their estate in France. Her father had done so after the war ended.

William assiduously scraped the bottom of the bowl with his spoon. "If Jacqueline is their daughter, she's one wealthy little girl." He frowned then grabbed a piece of the soft bread and sopped up the remainder of the liquid.

Christy wiped his patrician mouth with a cloth. "We need to find out if Pierre was trading with the fort at Michilimackinac during that time."

"And if he traded there that summer when the voyageurs first arrived." William grabbed another piece of squaw bread.

Shad fisted his hands. "Father Menard said Pierre was."

Across the table, Mercy caught his eye, sorrow painting her face. "We should bring her here, Shad." Mercy gestured around the cabin. As if she belonged there, too.

He and Little Fawn had known the sorrow of being childless, but he'd never have stolen another person's baby, as Pierre may have done.

Colonel Christy cleared his throat. "I lost my son many years ago, as you know, Shad."

Prickles covered Shad's arms. Natives from Little

Fawn's tribe had brought William and Shad out of a renegade Shawnee camp and north to safety.

"I'd exhausted every lead I had." The colonel's eyes glistened. "We owe it to the Beaujeu de Villemondes to make inquiries."

And to keep Jacqueline safe, as William had done when rescuing Shad. "I will fetch Jacqueline from the village in the morning."

But would they let her go?

Chapter 5

Morning song outside the cabin, an aviary sonata, woke Mercy early. Now, after serving the men a cold meal to break their fast, she'd cleaned up and prepared to leave. A buzz of excitement coursed through her at the notion of meeting little Jacqueline.

"Ready?" Shad moved to stand behind her.

"Yes."

He raised Mercy's red wool cloak to her shoulders, his fingertips touching her shoulders, heat blazing through her. Did little Jacqueline possess a warm coat? How Mercy longed to have her own children. If the child stayed with them, wouldn't it be like having their own little family? She and Shad and Jacqueline.

Scents of burnt hardwood, roasted venison, and damp leather goods permeated the cabin. She turned toward him catching his own unique scent of cedar and the bayberry soap she made for him each winter. She'd found several soap balls nestled in the bottom of his trunk. Each year she had anticipated Shad's visit with her and Father and she'd make a special batch for him. A smile tugged at both of their lips.

"Are you sure you want to come with us? 'Tis a long walk."

"Positive."

"I'm glad you kept this covering all these years." He clutched her shoulders, his thumb stroking the fine red wool of the cape.

She frowned. "Why wouldn't I? It's the prettiest clothing I own."

"I'm glad you think so. Little Fawn told me that my 'Penn's country' sister must have a warm covering."

In confusion, she searched his blue eyes. He was serious. The cloak he'd brought her years earlier had fed the moths some time back. Should she tell him? As she continued to gaze up at him, his features softened and his eyes widened. He leaned toward her. Was he going to kiss her?

William barged through the door, arms full of wood. "I see you have my cloak on, Mercy!"

Releasing her arms, Shad turned toward the other scout. "I bought her this cape some time ago, at Little Fawn's request, as well you should remember."

Shad's angry tone surprised her. Mercy reached out to touch his arm, her fingers grazing the muscles now forming again.

"I'm afraid that wonderful warm covering is gone." As was his dear wife. "This cloak was brought from Williamsburg by the colonel and William."

Christy strode through the door displaying two rabbits. "You look lovely in red, Mercy."

Shad's fists were balled as though he might strike someone. What was wrong with him?

An unreasonable fury burned through him. "And the cloak I bought you?"

Her dark eyebrows pulled together. "Oh, the moths ate that long ago—before I began using the cedar you brought to me."

Little Fawn had encouraged him to bring other gifts, some she'd made herself, and all had been displayed on the Clarke's fireplace mantel.

She stroked the cape. "That lovely cedar kept the little beasties from devouring this lovely garment. Leaning up on

70

her tiptoes, she kissed his cheek. "Thank you—and I loved that cloak so much, the first one. . ."

Mercy's pretty face reddened and she blinked at him several times. ". . .that William and Colonel Christy purchased another for me in Williamsburg when they last traveled through Virginia."

Lee Christy gave a chuckle and glanced at Shad. William shook his head and put the wood near the fireplace. Relief eased through Shad as though he'd just emerged from a scouting expedition, unscathed. But the Christy men weren't his enemies. They, like Little Fawn, also cared for this dear sweet woman and wanted to keep her safe and warm.

"Time to go check on the girl." William cracked his knuckles.

"Please, let's bring her back here no matter what they say to dissuade us." Mercy took several steps across the bear rug, spread on the wood planked floor, toward William. "Until we know more about her true parents."

Lee Christy, seated in a chair at the table, wrapped the leather that tethered his walking boots to his calves. "Who will care for her when we leave?"

Unmarried, her father missing, here only to affirm that Shadrach Clark, their valued scout and friend survived. Mercy swallowed. And possibly only on the island for a short while. She opened her mouth, but no sound emitted. She wasn't Shad's wife.

"We will." Shad's warm voice, behind her, sent tingles up her back.

William laughed. "Who is 'we'?"

Shad's eyes pierced her own. What was he asking?

Silence filled the cabin and they departed.

Miles later, Mercy rued that they'd walked through the interior rather than canoed around. The men did not wish to be in a canoe should they encounter the Chequamegon on the water.

"Next time you'll wear a proper type of moccasin." Shad wrapped an arm around her and squeezed Mercy's shoulder, sending a shiver through her.

Her feet ached in a rhythm that matched the sound of the waves lapping the nearby shore.

"I'll line them with the rabbit fur." William turned and flashed his white teeth.

Shad scowled. "Will take too long—I've got furs all cured in the loft."

She'd slept on those glorious furs the previous evening. Seemed a pity, the men all making do downstairs. Shad had slept on the floor on a stack of furs, when there were two mattresses in the loft, covered in furs, and a beautiful quilt their friend, Suzanne Rousch, had made for William long ago. But how often did he stay there? And her own pitiful attempt at a quilt—one she'd made for Shad. Where was it? Mercy chewed her bottom lip.

Catching a whiff of spruce that carried on the breeze, and the tangy odor of fish, Mercy hesitated.

Shad stopped. "Hungry?"

Her stomach growled.

Colonel Christy laughed, bringing up the rear, and patted his flat midsection. "I miss Rosa's good cooking."

William must have heard, for he snorted and swiveled around. "She's got nothing on Sarah's baking—her bread is the best anywhere."

And Mercy—what was her specialty?

Shad brushed her hair from her eyes. "Your roasts are what I miss—with tender little carrots and peas and beans cooked in the broth."

Her garden had just been put in. Could it grow without her watchful eye for weeds? And what of her father? "Thank you, Shad."

His brow puckered. "What ails you—besides the need of good food?"

Averting his gaze, she stared down at her flimsy, though pretty, shoes.

"I will trade for a pair of sturdier moccasins in the village. We're almost there." He lifted her from the ground, startling her and she threw her arms around his neck. When he turned and settled her in his arms, she struggled.

"Put me down." Though it wasn't proper, his embrace still felt wonderful, like the sunshine that peaked above the tree line this day. "You need to get your strength fully back."

William exhaled loudly, turned around, and continued to hike onward. Colonel Christy passed them and shook a finger at Shad. "I don't know that you've ever been quite restrained enough around women, Mister Clark."

"Ah, but he's wrong," Shad whispered into her ear. "And I'm just beginning to remember who I am. Who I was. And you've brought my strength back to me."

The boy who Shad had been, the son of the preacher, sent with by his parents with his aunt and uncle to the colonies—could Mercy find that boy and bring him back to the man? Shad blinked back the moisture gathering in his eyes and set Mercy back on her feet. He'd get one of the villagers to trade him moccasins for the promise of one of his pelts. And he'd for sure and for certain replace Mercy's cloak from William with a new one as soon as he could with the traders at Michilimackinac—if they came this year, that was. And if Pontiac's followers didn't join forces and do something foolish.

When they finally reached the village, Shad scanned the groups of children to see if the little blonde girl played amongst them. Near a fire, over which roasted small game, Jacqueline nestled on an elderly woman's lap. When William strode forward, the child rose but then blinked in confusion. William's dark hair and eyes and light complexion were much like the trapper, Pierre, who had raised the girl. Her gaze alighted on the colonel and then moved to Shad.

Raising her thin arms, which looked like two slim birch branches beneath her trading blanket, pinned at her long neck, she ran to Shad. "Monsieur Le Clerc, Monsieur. You have come for me."

The child's pleas plucked at his heartstrings much as William's fiddle music did. Jacqueline threw herself into his arms and he lifted her overhead, her sapphire eyes sad but then widening in glee.

She smiled, revealing perfect pearl-like teeth. What a beautiful little girl—and where were her true parents? The French girl was like a little jewel—a lost gem from a family who, by all accounts, had done little to look for her. He would have heard, had the commander had his child stolen. Why would they have suppressed such information?

Several of the younger braves in the tribe gathered around the colonel and his son, and were talking animatedly. Shad longed to join them. He lowered Jacqueline and patted her silken head.

Mercy bent and placed a hand on the girl's pink cheek.

Shad knelt beside her.

In French, he explained to the child, "Mercy is my friend."

The little girl glanced at Mercy, who nodded.

Mercy touched Shad and then pointed to herself. "*Amis.* Friends. We wish for you to come stay with us." Her cheeks turned crimson as Shad translated the last part for her.

The child threw herself against Mercy, whose eyes brimmed with tears as she offered him a tremulous smile.

A week now and the Chequamegon had not paddled around the island nor had the villagers had contact with them. The Christy men had taken the canoe that morning to circle the island once more.

Mercy knelt by the water. With so much washing to do, she and Jacqueline had carried the child's tiny garments as well as her own, Shad's, and the Christys'. At the shoreline she'd scrubbed them clean with soft soap from the women in the village. She smiled at the recollection of their assumption that she was Shad's new wife.

"Merci?" The tiny golden-haired girl, seated beside her on the new grass, rose. "*Bateau.* Boat!"

Jacqueline pointed to William, seated in the front of a canoe with the colonel in the back. Three soldiers accompanied them, their red coats bright against the cobalt water and the ivory birch bark of the vessel.

Feeling her jaw hanging slack, Mercy clamped her mouth shut and straightened, taking the child's hand. "We should go tell Shad."

"*Oui,* I go." The child ran off before Mercy could stop

her.

The five men were soon ashore and she'd returned to standing there gaping at them, though she knew not why. She'd seen soldiers before. But she'd not expected any to arrive on this island.

"Miss Clarke!" The colonel's spine couldn't have been straighter as he addressed her, having removed himself from the cluster of men. He'd been very formal with the commanders at Fort Detroit and Fort Michilimackinac when they'd been en route, but he'd been so angry at both posts that he'd not held that air of authority he displayed around his subordinates—as he did now.

The other men carried the canoe up onto the embankment. Christy cocked his head to the side as he approached her. Worry niggled in her gut.

"I've word of your father." He patted his slender hands against his thighs.

She much preferred him in buckskins than in his full regalia. And she'd rather he wore a smile than a frown.

"As you know, there's a troublemaker named Pontiac stirring up the confederation against the British." He gazed out to the gently rippling water. "As I've warned these people—they need to change the way they are dealing with the Iroquois and the others." His low voice held suppressed rage.

"And my father?" Mercy inquired.

Almost clear gray eyes met her own. Perhaps in his late forties, the man appeared almost ageless, his prematurely silver hair a contrast to the youthfulness of his handsome face. "Pontiac and his rebels claim they have him."

Dizziness encompassed her, whirling her like the eddies in the streams nearby. "Have him?" Her mouth forced the words out.

Colonel Christy patted her shoulder lightly. "They won't dare harm him."

Mercy sucked in a breath. "Why not?"

"Because they know Gray Badger—as I am known to the natives, and Lightfoot—my son's Native name, and Shadrach Clark are Reverend Clarke's good friends. *Ses bons amis*." His patrician features tightened, his face forming a stern mask.

"But.." What if they'd taken Father precisely because of this association? She didn't want to say so, would ask Shad what he thought.

"Colonel?" An enlisted man with his auburn hair pulled tightly back in a queue, removed his tricorn hat and bowed toward her.

"Go with my son, men." His curt words held no room for question.

Christy turned to face the soldier and motioned toward William, at the head.

The four formed a single file as they took to the path and left them, with William closest to her. "Mercy, it's possible Pontiac and his band took your father as a warning, though."

As she suspected. She tried to swallow her fear, but her throat squeezed tight.

Colonel Christy's sigh cut through the still air. "But I don't believe them at all."

Water lapped gently against the canoe, positioned nearby. "Why not?" she asked.

He rubbed his chin. "Because we never heard anything. Our allies would have told us."

From what Mercy had seen she wasn't sure the British had any allies this far north. "Why do they lie?"

"To send us on a wild goose chase after them, I

suppose." He gave a dry laugh and glanced overhead, as geese headed north.

"They wish us to leave here?"

"Perhaps." He lifted the toe of his shiny black boot, digging the heel into the sand. "If we leave and give up warning the forts of possible attack then they might become complacent again."

They'd not seemed to heed his and William's warnings as it was—already seemed nonchalant. "Shall you?"

Christy stared out across the water toward Michilimackinac. "Shall I…?"

"Leave? Stop warning them?" Though little good it seemed to do.

"Hmmm, perhaps." He tipped his head back and rubbed his neck, grimacing.

"But, sir—they didn't listen to you…"

His dark eyebrows drew together. "True enough."

They both stood on the shore. Across the straits, the English commander and his soldiers failed to acknowledge the colonel's recommendations. Had even laughed off that the Odawa people were unhappy, pointing out how content the people encamped around them seemed to be.

"The people here, the Chippewa village—do you trust them?"

"Yes, but with some reservations. Mercy—they agree that Pontiac is stirring up the people and that many will join him. I suspect the Chequamegon, who traveled so far— from the very end of Lake Superior— may do so. Those on the island and in Epoufette, Little Fawn's tribe and others nearby, however, shan't. They cannot say as much for their brethren below the straits, however."

One of little Jacqueline's dresses, caught by the breeze, lifted from the top of Mercy's laundry pile.

"The child, Colonel—have you word of her parents?"

Color drained from his face and he removed his hat before lowering himself to sit on a nearby boulder.

"What is it?"

"Several women from the settlement by Michilimackinac say the infant was left in the care of a French maid when the mother became ill. She brought the infant to the Rendezvous at the shore."

"Surely someone saw her."

"She had the babe hidden in a woven basket, cover with a light cloth." He shrugged. "One of the women said the caretaker wished to see her brother, who was coming in from Montreal."

"And someone took that opportunity. . ." Her hand slipped to her heart and Mercy looked to the trail where little Jacqueline emerged, held high over Shad's head.

"Pierre was seen carrying a woven covered basket to his bateau, and the women assumed he'd already made his trades and was carrying his goods home to his wife. And his boat indeed held new blankets and cloth from Quebec.

Her heart went out to the parents of the lost girl, now presumed to be Jacqueline. How, sir, could we get word to the suspected parents? How is that possible?"

The child had known nothing but rustic life—that of a child of a fur trader and trapper and his wife.

"I will send word when I return to Philadelphia." Colonel Christy bent and dipped his hands in the clear water. "But I don't know what to do until then."

Did he wish to wash his hands of the girl?

Chapter 6

Sizzling bacon puffed up clouds of smoky scent where Shad set to cooking. Mercy arched an eyebrow. "You're really not going to let me help?"

Shad stirred the coals beneath his cookfire outside the cabin. "No. Again, I say no." He squatted and poked at the thick slabs of pork fat with the long-handled fork, the implement's black twisted handle smoking. He turned from the fire and grinned at Mercy and at Jacqueline, who was throwing pebbles toward the path that led to the shore. The child loved the water. Or was she looking for someone? Perhaps for Pierre and Angelique to return for her. A breeze rustled the oaks and pines nearby, carrying the fragrance of new growth.

"Thank you for cooking." She rubbed her arms—hadn't worn her cloak outside because the afternoon had been warm, as was the cabin. With the sun moving lower in the horizon, chill set in.

Shad leaned away as fat popped on the griddle. "Didn't want either of you to get burned."

Papa, despite the loving man he was, never concerned himself as to whether what she prepared might be a hazard to her health. She had two good-sized scars to prove it—having removed a too-heavy pot of boiling water once and having been burned by grease another time.

"I've seen your scars over the years, Mercy." His soft voice was accompanied by a slow half-smile. "Ain't likely to let you get too close to hot fat on my watch."

She tugged at her sleeves, trying to cover where the marks began. Did he consider them unsightly? How had he noticed? Unless he was looking at her closely—as he was right now. Swallowing, she glanced at the cabin. "So, the others will not return tonight?"

He followed her gaze. "No, they'll likely not."

Mercy's cheeks warmed. "We'll be alone. Except for Jacqueline."

"Will be like we're a little family tonight." There was a tremor in his voice she'd only heard a few times before—when he'd spoken of his own family.

She looked up and caught the sheen on his eyes. He'd missed them so badly that he had wanted to believe she was his sister all those years ago. What about Papa—was he missing her, too? Guilt panged her heart, for while she was concerned for his well-being, she'd not lamented their separation in her heart. She knew her father loved her, but his world revolved around the Lord and around serving the backwoods people of Pennsylvania and Virginia. Her shoulders slumped.

"I wonder where my father is." And if they'd be able to remain on Mackinac.

Shad lifted several pieces of the fatback from the pan and laid them in strips on a nearby platter. With her beans, cooking inside over the hearth, they'd have a hearty meal. And she'd prepared cornbread, too.

"Reckon your father is safe." His warm eyes reassured her.

She wished he was right. "How do you know?"

"We'd have heard by now—Christy still has army, militia, and scouts about the countryside. Especially if someone had deliberately harmed him."

Like the people Christy mentioned?

"But I thought that person claimed they had abducted him."

"Pshaw! I don't believe that for a moment, that Pontiac and his men have him. I'm betting Rosa and her bunch will find him holed up with one of his church families in the mountains. But he might be ill, Mercy—maybe as ill as I was."

But Shad had almost died. "Why do you think that?"

"A hunch. Illness was coursing through the backwoods before I last saw you, and that was where your Father was headed. And I succumbed after being in your area."

"I see." But she didn't follow his logic at all.

His blue eyes darkened. "Do you miss him bad, Mercy? Are you planning to return with him to Pennsylvania?"

His Adam's apple bobbed.

She didn't miss her life at home. And she regretted so. While worried about Father, he'd been absent so much of her life—he reminded her of a shadow. Pivoting away, she wiped at her eyes and scanned for where Jacqueline had gone. She spied the girl bent, picking up pieces of driftwood.

"I'll go get her. It's time for dinner."

After retrieving the child and coaxing her home—or rather to Shad's cabin—Mercy moved toward the building, the thin smoke tendrils from the chimney beckoning her. Her heart began to pick up pace as the child ran toward the door. *No one but the three of us here. Alone. All night.*

Her breath caught in her chest as she lifted her skirts, revealing the fur lined moccasins that William and Shad had made for her. Comfortable and warm, they were like a loving embrace—something she longed for but rarely received from her father. And now, each night, she slept upstairs in the loft and wondered what it would be like to be encircled in Shad's arms all night. To sleep in his bed. To be his wife. She placed a hand on her chest, suddenly warm. Sucking in a breath, she stepped over the threshold, after Jacqueline.

"Smells good! *Bien*." The little girl picked up a plate from the table and held it out for Shad to fill. He ladled beans over strips of bacon.

Mercy uncovered the crock of butter from the village and also the cornbread and brought it to the oak table and seated herself on the trestle bench. Her heart fluttered as Shad filled her plate and set it before her.

"Thank you." No man had ever served her before, save the colonel.

"You're surely welcome." He grinned at her and then Jacqueline.

"Merci," Jacqueline said around a mouthful of beans. She'd not waited for a blessing nor had she placed a napkin in her lap. Could it possibly be that this beautiful little child truly was the daughter of a wealthy landowning family in France? All she knew was that tonight—this night—felt like a new beginning. Like the start of something much bigger than each of them—the birth of a family.

"You, too, little miss."

Jacqueline scrambled up the hillside—to the highest point near the harbor. Colonel Christy jabbed his walking stick into the grass as Mercy and Shad followed behind.

"'Tis the promontory point we need in order to observe."

"Eventually we'll need a fort here—I feel certain of it." Christy turned and faced the harbor, and the nearby village.

Mercy continued upward, keeping her skirts lifted above her moccasins but the weight of her petticoats an encumbrance—time to do without them. She paused and wiped perspiration from her brow as the sun beat down on her.

Shad reached for her hand, his fingers warm and sure as they wrapped around her own. "If a fort is built here we'd have a better chance at being able to support ourselves on the island. We could have a good life here, Mercy."

Her mouth went dry. Dare she imagine them living out their life together in this beautiful place? They mounted the slope and when they reached the top, Shad turned her to face the water. Brilliant sun shone off the deep azure expanse. In the far distance, structures of Fort Michilimackinac's denizens dotted the shoreline—both Ojibway and Odawas. Below them a field of green grass and wildflowers gently rocked in the breeze.

Shad wrapped his arms around her and pulled her back against him, his chest warm and solid.

"Beautiful, isn't it?"

He kissed the top of her head, sending frissons of warmth to her toes.

"Yes," her breathless agreement silenced when he pulled her more tightly to him as Jacqueline ran by, laughing.

Shad released her and the child pointed at them. "*L'amour*—like Mama and Papa." Although she smiled, Jacqueline's lips quivered and she ran to Colonel Christy, throwing herself against his buckskinned legs.

Mercy did love this man, this former scout. But he'd not actually asked her to marry him. Had he decided to live as the colonel and Rosa did—without the benefit of a marriage license or even a wedding blessed by the church? She wouldn't do so. Shad must make his vows before God. Had he ever made peace with the Lord he blamed for taking his family? Her stomach churned. A marriage without the blessing of God was no marriage.

Again, tonight, Mercy, Jacqueline, and he sat alone outside the cabin, pink fingers of sunset waving goodnight over the treetops. Shad whittled another clothes pin for the line. Seemed poor Mercy was constantly scrubbing something clean. He'd trade for new clothes and more soap on the morrow.

His lovely Mercy set her stitching down in her lap, yet another of his tunics that she'd repaired. "Would you play the fiddle for us?"

Her hazel eyes pleaded yet she also cast nervous glances toward the cabin. Lately she seemed downright jumpy to be with him and Jacqueline at night. He could fix that—make her his wife. Warmth coursed through him. He set the pin and his knife aside and grazed her smooth cheek with the back of his hand. Instead of pulling back from him, she covered his hand with her own cool one and leaned closer toward him.

"*Oui*. Play." The tiny girl brought William's violin case to Shad. She was beginning to speak more English.

Shad chuckled and stood. "You two gals got me wrapped round your little fingers." He demonstrated what he meant, pantomiming the gestures, and Jacqueline giggled but pushed the violin toward him. William's violin. Young Christy's second fiddle.

Shad's joy slipped away. He'd always been second to William, not being Christy's son. But he'd been the premier scout, no doubt of that, though William was a respected scout in his own right. Now, with Mercy and Jacqueline here, he had no desire to scout again. He wanted nothing more than to love and care for this woman, this child, too, if need be. Yet they may have to abandon this paradise if the area was attacked.

With love in her eyes, Mercy pressed his hand to her cheek and then released it. "You have the gift of bringing emotion from each piece—especially the Scottish ones you play. And in that respect William can't compare—those reels you play—he cannot match you."

He dipped his chin, acknowledging her compliment then he opened the case and drew out the fiddle and its bow. He ran a finger over the smooth wood. Could he allow William first place as scout, also—yes. Was William the better fiddler—yes, if one asked for classical violin pieces.

He sensed the Holy Spirit's presence in this room— whose voice Shad had run from for a decade. Until now.

"The Flowers of Edinburgh," he announced as he ran the bow across the strings and made adjustments.

Mercy clapped her hands in time to the music and Jacqueline lifted her skirts and danced while he played. He grinned at their merriment.

Shad played several more songs, pausing in between to throw a log on their small fire. The venison stew called to him from within the house, his stomach rumbling louder than his music. The child ceased dancing and ran behind him, but not before he spotted the unexpected movement in the bushes. Shad set down his violin and reached for his tomahawk and knife, strapped to him. His gun, set across the table moments earlier now rested on Mercy's shoulder.

"Stop right there!" She called out, her eyes fierce and her hands steady.

Two bent, filthy, buckskinned men half-dragged another man between them, followed by a woman. The three redcoats bringing up the rear gave Shad his ease.

"Put down the gun, Mercy." Those men hadn't even the

strength to hail the house. Shad rushed to them.

Mercy lowered the rifle with shaking hands, setting it on the slatted table and raised a hand to her mouth. "Father!"

Although his hair hung strewn about his shoulders, and his head bent away from her, Mercy recognized the vest she'd constructed for her father months earlier. As well as the boots Shad had brought on his last visit.

Reverend Jonathan Clarke's frock coat hung loose about his gaunt frame. He'd lost a stone or more weight.

Christy's woman, Rosa, walked behind them, her huge dark eyes filled with sorrow.

"What happened to him?" Mercy moved closer.

Shad ducked in between the other men and lifted her father up. He'd certainly regained his strength—perhaps Father would do the same, she prayed.

William shook his shoulders. "The renegades made an example of him. Pontiac told the truth—he did have him—had his braves take your father in Virginia and then run him to different camps telling the commanders that they'd all end up captive like your father—or dead if the English didn't mend their ways."

She followed Shad into the cabin, where he lowered Father gently onto the bed. "I'll get more water to boil and the soap. You get the cloths and then we men will clean him up proper once you tend to his face and neck."

Her father, a clean and genteel man, lay pasty white in filthy clothes, his hair greasy and matted to his head. Tears filled her eyes.

Rosa joined her. "I'm so sorry, Mercy—it took us a long time to track your father down. This time, they were able to hide their deeds. I had to trade many horses." Rosa looked away.

There was no way Mercy could repay the woman's kindness.

"I am very grateful."

"You would have done the same for me, for my Christy." Her dark eyes looked past Mercy toward the cabin door.

Had she the means, yes—Mercy would have. "Thank you for your kindness to me and my father."

Father inhaled a shuddering breath, his chest raising beneath her hand and then he coughed.

"Cool water for now." Shad set the bucket on the floor but hung the other on the grate to heat.

She dipped clean rags in the cold water and ran the first one over the soap. Turning to her father, she dabbed at the dirt on his face and the sores near his mouth.

Tears began to stream down her face. She couldn't abandon her father. When he was well she'd return with him to Pennsylvania and care for him like the good daughter she was. He had no one else.

Rosa tapped her arm and then sat beside her, washing her father's hands, so flat-looking now.

"Mercy, you should know something else."

"Yes?"

"There was a woman they took, along with your father. And he will be asking about her when he awakes."

A woman? "Who?"

"A widow from the Shenandoah Valley. A fine woman involved in the church ministry there. They took her with them, too."

Dear God, no.

"We left her at the fort in Michilimackinac—she was too

ill to bring across the straits."

Mercy's tears dropped onto her father's face, making rivulets in the dirt caked on him.

"They are wed, my dear." Rosa patted her hand.

Chapter 7

Shad wiped Reverend Clarke's brow with a clean cloth and then blotted it dry. The older man's face had relaxed as he'd entered deep sleep from the herbal draught William had given him. Now the preacher's deep even breaths filled the small alcove where the bed was situated.

Rising from the bed, he viewed Mercy, sound asleep on a pile of furs nearby. She'd begged to watch over her father, but the excitement of the day and her fatigue incapacitated her. Little Jacqueline had an arm draped around Mercy, whom she'd taken to like as a second, nay a third mother. Poor child. And if she truly was the French commander's daughter, what then?

After pulling his lone wing chair closer to the bed, Shad lifted his long legs up and covered them with the quilt Mercy had made him so long ago. He'd snuck it from upstairs when the men went up, not wanting them to soil it. Now all the men, save Christy, slept upstairs, elbow to elbow, in the loft. He couldn't get comfortable, though, and lowered his legs to the floor.

Shad's moccasin-clad feet remained silent as he slid across the planked floor and the skin rug to the door. Swiftly, he moved outside and beneath the full moon.

The colonel's silver hair glinted in the moonlight. "Beautiful isn't it?"

"Aye, 'tis." He'd hoped to bring Mercy out here tonight, beneath this very moon, and talk with her. Get a better feeling about whether she'd be willing to be his wife. Though he wasn't yet willing to ask. With his history of losing those he'd loved, he wanted a sign sure and for certain from God that Shad should ask. He swallowed.

The man's sly grin was at odds with his usual serious

nature. "Do you want advice?"

Shad's laugh began low in his belly and then worked its way up. "Christy, since when have you asked me if I wanted your opinion? Seems you've always offered it up easily—sometimes with a pretty little bow on it and others with tough pemmican to swallow with it."

Lee Christy's soft laugh was chased by an owl's soft hoot in the night. "You're a man now."

"And widowed."

"Little Fawn was a good woman."

"She was."

"Mercy knows you well. Like Rosa understands me." Silver eyes, like a wolf's, glittered. "And when her father recovers he has his own wife to tend to now. Two women in the same household, two grown women, have a hard time of it—especially when one is a stepmother. Which is one reason I sent Rosa to Pierre's cabin, which is where we'll be staying."

"I see." He'd not had the chance to see how his sister, Rachel, had grown up and how she'd managed with their mother.

"You would do well with her at your side."

"You know I'd give up scouting altogether, though." And hadn't the search for his parents been a large part of his drive to become a scout?

The colonel reached into his leather pouch and retrieved his pipe and a packet of tobacco. He tamped down the leaves and then struck his flint several times until he ignited the pipe.

"I hadn't thought I'd ever marry at all, but Little Fawn wore me down with her gentle persistence."

The colonel chuckled. "And her clear preference of you over any of the men in her tribe."

"In the end, she'd won. Yet Little Fawn had been taken from him, too, like the rest of his family—leaving him alone once more.

"You're a man who shouldn't be alone."

Christy seemed to speak the very same words God was putting into his heart.

The colonel scratched at his forehead. "Not sure why exactly I said that, but it rings true. And Mercy loves you, you know."

What was he afraid of? Of all the women he'd known, Mercy reminded him most of his own mother and the women in his family in England and of the church folk who'd surrounded him as a child. Yet they'd deserted him. Sweat broke out on his brow. No…his mother hadn't deserted him—they'd trusted his aunt and uncle to take him to the colonies and prepare the way for them when they arrived. But they'd never arrived. And his uncle had died on the trip over, his aunt quickly married the brutal man responsible for her death. Or was he, Shad, the one responsible? Could he have saved her? He ran a hand through his hair and pulled the tie from his queue.

"I've also wanted to speak to you, of word Rosa received from Colonel McCready on her way here."

The man called "Badger" for his ferocity, assumed a decidedly gentle stance. "McCready had a lieutenant who'd requested that his wife and children join him. She'd been raised in England, the daughter of a preacher. He had concerns."

The hairs on Shad's arms stood on end. "And?"

"McCready refused. But he made inquiries about Rachel."

Shad's heart stuttered. "Rachel?"

"Seems her father, Reverend John Clark, pastors a

church in upstate New York."

The air rushed from Shad's lungs. "And her mother?"

"There with her father. Her name is Anne."

After all this time, could it be? He drew in a steadying breath. "And you've not spoken of these inquiries to me until now?

Colonel Christy stiffened. "I refrained until I felt there was more than a modicum of truth—and secondary affirmation."

"Is there now?"

"Clark—McCready told Rosa he'd seen a portrait the lieutenant sketched of his beautiful wife. It included a blurred shadow indicating a large half-moon-shaped scar that marred her porcelain brow—that is exactly what he said."

"And he confirmed her parents' names."

"Yes."

"And they are alive?"

"Indeed. And McCready did the decent thing and sent both the lieutenant's wife and her parents letters telling them about you." Christy coughed. "Of course, he left out the part about he wasn't' quite sure where you were. He directed them to address correspondence to you in care of me to my Philadelphia residence."

"Why there?"

"I think I've earned a respite after all these years, and the army agrees, too. And McCready thought if your family could travel to Philadelphia that I'd have room for them in my home.

"I see." Woodsmoke puffed up from the chimney—competing with the officer's pipe smoke. The colonel's grand home was nothing like the other places Shad had made his home over these long years.

A moment of doubt crept in. "Sir, did McCready ask the lieutenant if she had a brother?"

Christy sent a series of exhaled pipe smoke heavenward. "That was a stumbling block, for he'd originally told Colonel McCready that she had three younger brothers. But when he inquired further, then he learned she had a missing older brother."

Three younger brothers? He'd not had any younger brothers.

"Her elder brother, Shadrach, disappeared with her aunt in the wilds of Virginia almost a score ago."

His chest constricted and Shad knelt on one knee. Could it be that after all these years he'd be reunited with his family? And he'd meet his younger brothers. All of this at a time when he had no idea what do about his own situation in life. One thing he did know, he couldn't live without Mercy in his life. And little Jacqueline had made a permanent place in his heart, too.

"I can't drag Mercy and the child so far away."

"Mercy is one of the strongest women I've ever met. It would take a wife like that to manage a husband like you will be to her. She would manage."

"I'd have to support her and Jacqueline, too. And I haven't quite worked that out." If they stayed, he could trap and fish and they could have a garden.

"You're forgetting that Jacqueline may have true parents elsewhere praying for her return, as your parents no doubt have." Christy assumed his take-charge military bearing. "We can bring Miss Clarke and Jacqueline with us—there's plenty of room at my house. And we'll figure things out from there. Would be good to give it some use with us gone so long from home."

Shad closed his eyes for a moment to pray. *God guide*

me.

In his spirit, he felt a check against leaving the child on the island. And an urging to make Mercy his wife. And to present her to his parents and sister. Could it possibly be true? After all these years?

Tomorrow. He'd speak with Reverend Clarke first and then with Mercy.

Several days had passed, with Mercy's father making a good recovery. But during that time Shad convinced himself that they'd need to leave the island soon, for safety, and that he had no means of supporting a wife. What would he do? He could no longer scout. And what if his parents wished for him to spend time with them? How would he leave a new bride behind? The trip to Philadelphia would be taxing—dare he ask a new bride to make such a trip? Now en route in a fur-laden canoe to Fort Michilimackinac, he regretted that he'd not trusted God to provide. He'd ask Mercy when they returned. Then they could wed as soon as they got her father home.

He dipped his oar into the water, feeling William's own sure stroke behind him.

"Did you ask her yet, Shad?"

He bowed his head and dipped harder, faster, almost upsetting the canoe. *Coward.* Sweat dotted his brow.

William coughed. "I guess you haven't asked Mercy to marry you then?"

Christy called out from the back, "Not necessary, William—Reverend Clarke has already demanded to perform the nuptials on the morrow."

"What?" Shad's voice was almost inaudible to his own ears over the sound of the waves.

The colonel continued, "Soon as he can stand. I say—

Shad you did know that you are marrying Mercy, didn't you?"

With his oar almost slipping from his hands, Shad caught it back up and sat, still, allowing the other men to paddle the boat forward. His heart beat a steady thump in his chest. *Lord, I asked You to answer my prayers, and you have.*

He laughed. "Well, then, I guess I didn't have to ask, did I, William?"

The other scout chortled and the colonel's guffaw carried forward. "Perhaps we should procure a gown while we are at Michilimackinac with the traders."

That and so much more. Fine furs lay stacked behind them. They'd get enough supplies to carry them easily to Detroit. And they'd make one last attempt at warning the commander at the fort to take notice and to deal more generously with the Ojibway and other tribes nearby. Tomorrow night—where would he and Mercy spend their first night as man and wife? His face flushed and he leaned toward his shoulder to wipe it. Those pretty lips would belong to his woman, his wife, and soon they would be one.

Mercy ceased fluffing her father's pillow filled with rags and cedar chips. "You told Shad what?"

"That I shall perform your wedding on the morrow."

Irritation prickled her arms. "Father—you cannot force him to marry me."

"Why not? I'm your father. He loves you and you love him."

"But…"

He raised a hand and began to cough. She pushed him

forward in the bed and patted his back, feeling his ribs beneath his flannel nightshirt.

"We've done nothing wrong, if that is what you fear." That was not altogether true. Stolen kisses, embraces, hand holding, lying aside one another. Were those not behaviors best saved for marriage?

Father raised one bushy eyebrow. "I've a new wife. You can't come home with me."

She sucked in a breath, anger filling her. Her father had made Mercy his home keeper for a decade, after her mother had died. She'd been forced into that role and as time had gone on, all the tasks and chores required had robbed her of the opportunity of beginning her own life. Until now. But to have him so bluntly speak these words, as though dismissing her from a job was almost too much to bear. "The men have gone to Michilimackinac to get that new wife back to you."

"Good." He closed his eyes.

"And then they'll see what should be done about getting you two…" She emphasized the last word, not including herself, for she'd decided she would stay on Mackinac with Shad and Jacqueline, and that he would marry her—she'd prayed about it and God spoke to her heart that she and Shad were to be yoked. So why was she angry with her father? It was the way he'd spoken his words. She felt used, as though she'd been nothing but a place holder for this new woman. "…home."

He opened his eyes and glared up at her. "Do you think I'd allow my daughter to stay behind with a man she's not wed to? Nay—you shall be wed on the morrow, whether either of you wishes it or not."

She did wish the marriage to occur. Was this her answer? She began to laugh until her eyes filled with tears.

She brushed them from her eyes as little Jacqueline ran to her and threw her arms around her.

The child kissed Mercy's cheeks. "*Un marriage?*"

"Yes!"

The little girl turned and kissed Father's bristly cheeks, unperturbed in the least that he'd not shaved.

"Better?" Jacqueline's brilliant smile did make everything better.

Father squeezed the child's arms. "You are a good little girl. *Tres bon, Tres bien femme.*"

Jacqueline kissed him again, laughed and ran outside.

French lace encircled the neckline of the dress which dipped rather low for Mercy's modest taste. The peach satin fabric enhanced her coloring.

Jacqueline had sighed and patted Mercy's cheeks, pronouncing, "*Tres belle marie.*"

If only Shad thought the same. They took him to Pierre's old cabin to change into his wedding clothes. She'd never seen Shad in full traditional men's clothing, since he'd normally worn buckskins.

Outside the cabin, the sounds of men speaking in hushed tones carried inside. Father had arrived.

She discerned Colonel Christy's words, "'Tis best we move this along Reverend, for we need to depart soon."

Leave? Soon? Mercy lifted her heavy skirts so she could go outside to ask but then dropped them again. What of her wedding night? Half of her wished to flee while the other half longed to spend the evening in her husband-to-be's arms. She drew in a long breath and then exhaled. If they were to all leave, then she'd not enjoy such luxury—not if they traveled again.

Jacqueline touched the beads that encircled Mercy's neck—a wedding gift from Shad, purchased at a trading post on Michilimackinac. She had nothing to give to him— save her heart.

"I now pronounce you husband and wife in the eyes of the church." Father closed his eyes. "Lord bless my daughter and new son. Bring happiness and joy into their lives. Keep them safe, especially on this coming journey."

Mercy opened one eye. Shad shifted beside her, his warm hand firmly grasping hers, possessive and sure. Journey?

"In Jesus's name, Amen."

With a swoop of his arms, Shad pulled her close and kissed her full on the mouth, in front of everyone. The men whooped and hollered and Mercy felt her cheeks burning.

"You're my wife," Shad whispered in her ear. "And I love you, Mercy. You've saved me. You found me and brought me back from the brink."

She pulled back from him. "Not me, Shad. But God— He saved you."

"Aye, He did." He tipped his head back, his hair glowing gold beneath the sun breaking through the piney bower. Intense blue eyes searched her face. "He saved me for you."

Mercy pressed her face against his shoulder and inhaled his unique scent of cedar, leather, and clean wool. She wanted to remember this moment forever, when she became Shad's wife.

Behind them, someone whistled loudly. "We have

company!"

Shad jerked away from her and whirled around, his hand reaching beneath his jacket, where his knife lay sheathed. Colonel Christy grabbed a rifle and William displayed two hatchets, one in each hand. Her eyes widened. Mercy's heart beat wildly. Was her wedding day to be marred by disaster? Were they under attack?

One of the soldiers at the edge of the group waved his tricornered hat overhead. "It's only Lieutenant Jamet and some soldiers."

Shad exhaled loudly and returned his knife to its holder. He wrapped his arm around Mercy. "He's an officer who'd been stationed in Sault Sainte Marie."

He'd told her about the small fort there having burned in the autumn.

Colonel Christy and William sent an unspoken message to Shad and he nodded at them. Both headed toward the visitors.

Father touched her shoulder. "You two should go ahead and start the feast. Enjoy your moment, my girl." He kissed her cheek.

Shad led her toward the wood table, laden with journey cake and butter, smoked fish, slices of ham, and a large apple tart sweetened with maple sugar. He filled a plate for himself and for her and nodded toward the wood stumps that would serve as their seats.

She sat and Shad soon joined her, grinning like a small boy who'd been allowed his first-ever purchase in a shoppe. Mercy couldn't help but be distracted by the presence of the newcomers, though. Why had they come?

Jacqueline ran to Mercy and planted a sticky kiss on her cheek. The child grabbed her hand and attempted to pull her up. "Monsieur Jamet *il sait*--he knows--my parents' *bons amis* dear friends—Cadottes."

"Cadottes?" The name was familiar, one Shad and the colonel had mentioned.

"Cadottes very good to me." A tear slid down her pale cheek.

Had Jacqueline expected them to come for her? Mercy frowned.

Shad bent down toward the child. "*Laissez Miss Mercy profiter de chaque journée spéciale*. Let Miss Mercy enjoy her special day, Jacqueline."

The girl blinked. "*C'est* Mistress Mercy now, Madame Mercy *non* Mademoiselle."

Shad laughed, but his eyes were serious. "*Nous parleron avec* Lieutenant Jamet. We will speak with him."

Jacqueline dipped her chin. "Oui, monsieur." She looked absolutely pitiful. The child had suffered so much already.

Rolling his eyes, Shad set aside his plate and stood. "Let's go see."

"I'd like to go, too." Mercy made to put her plate down as well but Shad motioned for her to stay.

When Jacqueline reached the area where the strangers were congregated she let out a shriek of delight as an officer with heavy burn scars on his neck and face stepped away from the others and opened his arms. He lifted the girl up in the air. So much for Shad's subtle warning that he would speak to the lieutenant, likely hoping that she'd infer that it was he who would do the talking.

Colonel Christy turned and looked at Mercy, unconcealed sadness dominating his features. He spoke something with William and Shad and then strode toward her. By the time he reached her, his face was a mask of determination. "That's Lieutenant John Jamet, the survivor of that fire in Sault Sainte Marie, and friend to Jean-

Baptiste Cadotte, whose home was the only one left unscathed."

Mercy nodded, clutching a knot of her wedding dress in her hand. "And he has news?"

Christy's lips pulled in tightly. "He does." He tapped his toe into the ground.

"He's brought a wedding gift perhaps?" She tilted her head at him and managed a curt laugh.

"In a way. He's brought advice from Cadotte."

"And that's a gift?"

"Aye, it is."

Mercy, wrapped in her red cloak, shivered in the long canoe despite the sun shining overhead this early June day. At Fort Michilimackinac, the rather young-looking Captain George Etheridge had dismissed Colonel Christy's concerns once more as he had ignored Jamet's and that of others. All was well, he'd insisted. Trader Alexander Henry had supplied them for their trip. Father's new wife, who seemed to be a sweet woman, rejoined them and sat farther back from Mercy.

Jacqueline squirmed in Mercy's lap.

The Cadottes had demanded, or rather requested strongly, that the girl be sent to them on a nearby island.

"They can protect her," Colonel Christy had insisted. "And she knows and loves them."

He'd also shared that the Cadottes had sent word to Jacqueline's true parents, confirmed as the former French commander of the fort and his wife. Perhaps they would send someone back for her or make some arrangement.

William continued paddling, frowning. "We should be to Bois Blanc soon."

And then Mercy would have to release this child of the Straits back to people she didn't know but who were purported to be highly influential. Lieutenant Jamet had brought the warning from the Cadottes that any English were unsafe there. They'd heard that Shad had an English woman now and he may no longer be protected. And they'd also advised that her father and his woman also leave the Straits of Mackinac, too.

These were influential people, used to getting their own way. Cadotte's wife was a relation of the chief Madjeckewiss, whom she'd shared with Jamet was influenced by Pontiac. There was more Jean-Baptiste would tell them when they met on the small island adjacent Mackinac. Still, shouldn't she and Shad have a say in what happened to Jacqueline?

They rounded the point of Mackinac Island and soon headed toward the southern tip of Bois Blanc. Gentle puffs of smoke wafted over the tree line near the shore. Near the front of the boat, Colonel Christy kept his head low as he worked, dashing his oar in and out of the water. Attired in Frenchman's work clothes, his head was covered in a faded reddish-pink wool knit cap. William and Shad were similarly attired. No buckskins for either. Gentle puffs of white clouds dotted the brilliant azure sky, hinting at a happiness of which Mercy was so unsure.

Soon, they were headed toward the shore and a small group of men, some clearly Frenchmen, some native, and some a mix or Métis, clustered there.

"Bonjour!" A strong-featured Frenchman called out.

"Monsieur Cadotte!" Jacqueline struggled to be free of Mercy's grip and would have thrown herself into the cold water to swim ashore if Shad hadn't stopped her. Soon, the canoe was pulled up onto the sand.

"We won't be here long," Colonel Christy warned them, as he assisted Mercy's new stepmother out.

"Take Jacqueline first," Mercy told Shad.

He took the girl to Cadotte, who grabbed her up and hoisted the laughing child into the air. A pang of jealousy swept over Mercy. But as Shad returned to her, his steps so confident, his health fully recovered, she couldn't be ungrateful toward God. The Lord had given her friend, now her husband, back to her and restored him. And if He willed it, they would begin their own family one day.

Shad helped her out, his hands firm, steady. "I love you, Mrs. Clark."

"I love you, Mr. Clark."

He bent and kissed her possessively. When they broke free he laughed. "I'm hoping one night soon we'll actually be alone and able to, well, you know…"

She felt her cheeks heat. But they were husband and wife after all. "I'm thinking a first night together packing things up and strategizing how to best leave the area, isn't the way most newly married couples start things."

"I'd agree." He kissed her again then took her hand and led her toward Cadotte and his men stood.

Cadotte set Jacqueline down and pointed toward a striped blanket covered with goods. "Go get some of the maple sugar candy."

The child ran off and the man's features tugged, as though he was struggling with emotion.

One of the younger men, with sleek dark hair pulled back into a queue and a mix of French and Ojibway features, nodded as if to encourage the older man. "I am the brother of Cadotte's wife. I came from Detroit to tell him of the attack there."

"When?" Colonel Christy moved closer to the Métis man.

"Not long after you departed. I saw you there at Fort Detroit with the woman." He pointed at Mercy.

"I didn't see you."

"You would not have." The man crossed his arms over his chest. "And what I tell you now is only for your safety. The people are not happy with the English disrespect of our ways. The French will return and restore order."

William shook his head, but Colonel Christy shot him a quelling glare.

Shad shifted beside her, his fingertips straying toward his knife. Did he fear attack? If so, why would they warn them?

Cadotte raised his hand. "We have been friends, Clark, for many years now. Heed my advice and do not stop on your journey only as you find necessary. Avoid Fort Detroit."

Cadotte's brother-in-law jerked his chin upward. "Stay away from Fort Michilimackinac now that you have the Black Robe's woman."

Father was not a priest, but Mercy wasn't about to say anything.

"I understand." Colonel Christy's two words bore the weight of so much more. "But are you not here for the child?"

Cadotte and his brother-in-law exchanged a quick glance. "That's what we told Jamet. I wish there was more I could say to him. He spent much time with my two young daughters, during his recovery."

His brother-in-law made a grunting sound. "And my sister is now with child again."

A smile tugged at Cadotte's lips. "I wanted you to know that I sent word to Commander Beaujeu de Villemonde after we heard of Pierre's and Angelique's deaths. And he never sent word back."

So, the Frenchman, or at least his wife, must have known what had happened but not acted on the information. A code of silence among the fellow Métis.

Colonel Christy shifted uneasily. "Are they in France with Geneviève's family? I can send word to them myself."

"It may be best if you initiate that contact. You are, after all, from an aristocratic land-owner's family and a fellow officer." Cadotte averted his gaze, frowning as he watched Jacqueline playing near the water.

Shad stepped forward. "I wish to take Jacqueline with me. With us—I am now married to Mercy, who has been caring for her. I know she'd love her like a mother if Beaujeu de Villemonde and his wife do not send for their daughter."

"Would you swear to bring Jacqueline back to us in time?" Cadotte's dark eyes bore into his. "You do plan to return, do you not?"

Did he? He wasn't sure. But glancing around at the turbulent Straits of Mackinac, something tugged at his soul. He nodded and he couldn't miss the wide-eyed glance he received from Mercy.

Cadotte's brother-in-law whispered something to him.

Cadotte squared his shoulders against his colorful cotton shirt. "You should know something. Detroit has been under siege since after you left."

Epilogue
Christmas, Philadelphia 1763

Mercy passed Shad her soft cotton handkerchief and he swiped at his eyes, grateful for this woman who had been part of God's plan to bring him full circle. His eyes hadn't been so blasted leaky, though, since he'd first arrived in the colonies, his uncle dead and he and his aunt on their own, and his family across the ocean. Now, though, his parents, sister and her family, and his younger brothers sat across from him at the Christy's grand mahogany table.

The scents of roasted goose and mashed potatoes and gravy accompanied two servants who carried trays to the massive sideboards. Baskets of rolls and crocks of butter occupied spots at each end of the table.

"Good thing this seats sixteen." Father pulled Mother's chair out and she slipped in, arranging her best gown around her.

"But we'll need to yell to be heard at the other end of the table," Rachel observed dryly.

Jacqueline sat at the end of the table, near Rachel and her family, the children still clutching their toys. Jacqueline's soft doll, hand-stitched by Mercy, had already been kissed a hundred times and named Angelique.

On his way to the head of the table, Colonel Christy paused and whispered in Shad's ear, "A good thing you didn't discuss Jacqueline's other parents with her."

A pang shot through Shad's heart. Beaujeu de Villemonde had replied to their inquiry. But he'd demanded positive proof that Jacqueline was indeed his child. He would not put his wife through the ordeal of being reunited with a child who may not be theirs. Beaujeu de Villemonde went on to describe in unflattering terms what he thought of the French and Métis countryfolk who inhabited the area. It was clear that he didn't wish to bring what he considered a peasant child into their grand home. When he had discussed the letter with the colonel, Shad felt relief, rather than anger. Was it selfish to be glad that he knew this child would be in his care until she grew into adulthood and made her own choices? Still, they'd agreed to send another correspondence to the former commander and invite him to meet them in Mackinac when Pontiac's War had finally settled.

Shad's three brothers sat to his father's, or rather their father's left. It seemed so strange to realize they truly were also his father's sons. Their resemblance to Shad was undeniable, with matching thatches of various shades of golden hair and blue eyes. But their wiry frames, unlike his own body, hadn't been ravaged by years scouting. He couldn't deny that he envied them that freedom from the aches and pains brought on by hard travel and sleeping out in the elements.

"You're staring again." His youngest brother, Edmund, complained.

Mercy, who'd just reentered the room, looked pale. She'd departed rather quickly when she'd first arrived, turned on her heel, and left. She went to Edmund and patted his shoulder. "He's thinking what a handsome lad you are and how grateful he is to have you here with us."

Mother looked up at Mercy, her new daughter-in-law, and beamed at her as she touched the creamy shawl that draped around her narrow shoulders. Mercy had worked on that shawl for weeks, after they'd arrived in Philadelphia.

His beautiful wife wound her way around the table, tapping each person there on the shoulder and speaking a word of encouragement. How had he been so blessed? Could his joy be any more complete?

When she reached him, Shad bent and kissed her cheek. Then he assisted her into the shield-backed chair. Was that his imagination or did she look horrified? Shad glanced around the room as the servants returned with platters of sliced ham and baked apples. Mercy pressed her hand to her mouth and appeared to be holding back a gag.

"What is wrong?"

Across the table, Mother pushed her seat back and Father rose to assist her. "Come with me, Mercy."

Rachel looked up from the children at the other end of the table.

Shad stood and helped Mercy up. He took her elbow and assisted her from the room. Mother moved ahead of them into the hallway, which was festooned with garlands of evergreens and holly berries. The scent of pine and mistletoe filled the hallway.

Mother motioned for Shad to return to the dining room. "Please tell the colonel to not wait on us as we'll be there shortly."

He dipped his chin and returned to his chair after conveying Mother's message. But now, seated at his place, a vast array of silverware and china dishes set before him, Shad's hands began to shake. His own illness had begun suddenly, and he'd been nauseated by food as his wife now was. God couldn't take Mercy away from him after he'd finally been reunited with his family. He blinked back more moisture from his eyes and loosened his cravat.

William, late to arrive, rushed in and took his place nearby, beside his wife Sarah and their sons. "What's wrong with you, Clark?"

"Nothing."

Sarah cocked her head at him. She'd known him a long time and had been through many ordeals with him, including being forted together during an attack on the Virginia frontier. "Are you upset that Mercy and I didn't cook the feast?"

That did pull a smile from him. He'd threatened William that if he one more time bragged about his wife's cooking then he'd make him do the job instead of the Christys' household staff.

From the end of the table, Shad's sister Rachel seemed to be smirking at him. Rachel whispered something into her husband's ear and both of them looked at him and laughed. They actually laughed. Anger welled up and he fisted his hands.

The pocket doors drew open again and Mother and Mercy returned. His wife clutched a small pouch, which she raised toward her nose and then squared her shoulder and lowered what must have been a packet of medicinal herbs.

The servants entered, both holding bowls of carrots and cooked greens.

Shad helped Mercy into her chair. "Are you all right, my darling?"

She grinned up at him. "Never better." But then she blinked rapidly and held the scented bag up to her nose.

Across from him, Mother sent him a knowing look and said something to Father, too quiet for him to hear.

"A Father?" Edmund scowled at their father. "Isn't he already a father to Jacqueline?"

Mercy grabbed and squeezed his hand. "I have another Christmas gift for you. But this one could take about seven months to arrive."

Shad sank into his seat.

His wife leaned in. "You'll need to have the seamstress add extra width to the front of the new red cloak that you ordered for me."

"Gladly!" He kissed her there in front of all these friends and family.

Guffaws and cheers erupted.

He'd been wrong. He could have been even happier and even more blessed. Who knew what else God could do in their lives?

The End

Carrie's Other Books

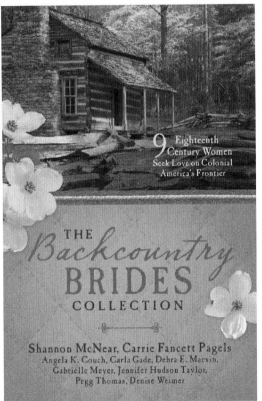

Thank you for reading *Mercy in a Red Cloak*! If you enjoyed this story you may wish to read Carrie's novella, "Shenandoah Hearts" in *The Backcountry Brides Collection* from Barbour Publishing (2018). Shad Clark makes an appearance in that story. Also, be sure to read author Pegg Thomas's novella, "Her Red Coat", in that collection, which is set at Michilimackinac during the attack.

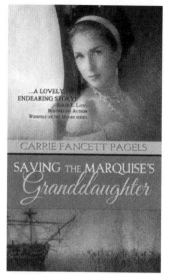

You'll also read about Colonel Christy and his son, William, in *Saving the Marquise's Granddaughter* from Pelican (2016), which received a Romantic Times Book Reviews 4 Star rating.

Carrie has many other books you can read, too! Check out her Books Page on her website at www.carriefancettpagels.com!

Author Bio

Carrie Fancett Pagels, Ph.D., is an ECPA bestselling and award-winning author of seventeen published inspirational historical romances, tagline "Hearts Overcoming Through Time."   Carrie's novel, *My Heart Belongs on Mackinac Island: Maude's Mooring* (Barbour, July 2017) won the **2018 Maggie Awards winner** for Novel with Religious Elements and was a ***Romantic Times Book Reviews* Top Pick**. Carrie's romance novella, *The Steeplechase*, was a finalist in the prestigious Holt Medallion Awards in 2017. Her short story, "The Quilting Contest", was the Historical Fiction **Winner of Family Fiction's *The Story* national contest** and published in a book by that name. Her novella, *The Substitute Bride*, was a 2016 Maggie Award (published) finalist for Romance Novellas. All three of her Christy Lumber Camp books were long list finalists for Family Fiction's Book of the Year and *The Fruitcake Challenge* was a Selah Award finalist.

Possessed with an overactive imagination, that wasn't "cured" by twenty-five years as a psychologist, Carrie loves bringing characters to life. She also teaches at writing conferences and seminars on "Why Back Story Matters" in character development. Brought up in Michigan's beautiful Upper Peninsula, Carrie resides with her family and their adopted Kelpie in the Historic Triangle of Virginia. Carrie enjoys reading, traveling, baking, and beading-but not all at the same time!

Website: www.carriefancettpagels.com

Blogs: Overcoming With God and Colonial Quills

Social Media Links:

Facebook Author Page

Facebook Personal Page

Twitter

Pinterest

goodreads

LinkedIn

Amazon author page

Bookbub

Instagram

Reviews Appreciated!

If you enjoyed Shad and Mercy's story, a review would be much appreciated!

If you'd like to keep up with Carrie and her books, sign up for her newsletter on her website's Contact Page. You'll receive updates on her books and notifications on upcoming events and giveaways.

Again, Thank you for reading my inspirational fiction! I'm a big fan of the following Christian historical romance authors (and I'm sure some I'm leaving off) and I encourage you to read their stories: Tamara Alexander, Debbie Lynne Costello, Susanne Dietze, Lena Nelson Dooley, Julie Lessman, Kathleen L. Maher, Serena Miller, Tracie Peterson, and Jen Turner Turano.

Made in the USA
Las Vegas, NV
08 December 2020